(megan) 3

(megan) 3

MARY HOOPER

BLOOMSBURY

First published in Great Britain in 2001
Bloomsbury Publishing Plc, 38 Soho Square, London, W1D 3HB

Copyright © Mary Hooper 2001

The moral right of the author has been asserted
A CIP catalogue record of this book is available from the
British Library

ISBN 0 7475 5503 6

Printed in Great Britain by Clays Ltd, St Ives plc

10 9 8 7 6 5 4 3 2 1

Thanks to Phil
for being a helpful PC wizard

'Megan! You're not putting him in that outfit,' Mum said. 'Please don't tell me you're putting him in *that* for his birthday party.'

'Yes, I am,' I said. We both looked at Jack. He was wearing a white Baby Gap T-shirt and denim shorts with studs around the pockets. 'I think he looks really sweet.'

'Sweet! The legs of his nappy are sticking out of the shorts and that T-shirt is too small, too tight around the arms and will be filthy by four o'clock. He looks really common – all he wants is an earring.' She frowned. 'Why don't you put him in that nice little yellow jumper I bought.'

'Per-lease,' I said.

Mum gave a great sigh. 'Well, you think you know best, of course. Far be it for me to interfere in my own grandson's upbringing.' And then she went on, trying to do just that. 'Clothes make a person, Megan. You dress to an image; how you want to be seen. If you dress Jack like a yob, he'll grow up like a yob. When you were little I dressed you up for parties. You had special clothes for parties. Always looked pretty.'

'Things have changed,' I said.

'Oh, they certainly have,' she said. 'And not for the better, either.'

Jack was sitting on the floor in our flat, surrounded by a coloured sea of wrapping paper that had held his presents. One year old that day, he had straight dark hair, blue eyes with long lashes, pink, plump cheeks and two teeth. As I stared at him, wondering how it was possible that he was really mine, he leaned forward, grabbed a corner of a crumpled sheet of red wrapping paper, and began to push it into his mouth.

'Get that off him!' Mum said. 'That'll be poisoned. Make him sick.'

'They wouldn't make wrapping paper that was *poisoned*!'

Mum put down the big iced sponge cake she was carrying and darted at Jack, snatching the paper away. 'I expect it's made in Hong Kong. They haven't got the same standards there.'

Jack gave a startled cry as she pulled the paper away from him. He turned, put out his bottom lip and looked at me sadly, his eyes filling with tears. 'Bye-

byes,' he said. What he meant was he wanted the grubby bit of blanket he always liked to hold when he was upset, or went to sleep. Before he could start crying properly, I picked him up and swung him on to my hip.

'Now see what you've done!' I said to Mum. 'It's unlucky to cry on your birthday.'

'Rubbish!' she said. 'Old wives' tales. I should say it was more unlucky to get poisoned by wrapping paper.'

I looked at her and just couldn't be bothered to argue. 'Yeah. Whatever,' I said.

Heaving a big sigh, I took Jack off to the bedroom we both shared with my sister Ellie. This was Mum's old bedroom, so still had horrible flowery wallpaper and pink shiny curtains. It was much too cramped for the three of us, of course – and it would be worse still in a few months' time, when Jack would need a proper bed.

I sighed again. I'd have to put up with it, though. And put up with Mum.

'I can hear her going on from here,' Ellie said. She was lounging on her bed with headphones hanging around her neck. A song I didn't recognise was coming out of them – not that I recognised much on the music scene nowadays. Since I'd had Jack I didn't seem to be able to keep up with things like that: music, boy bands, fashion, whatever was cool. Somehow I seemed to have stopped being a teenager. Ellie, who wasn't yet thirteen, was more of one than I was. Exactly what *I* was, I wasn't sure. I didn't seem to fit in anywhere.

'Mrs Nagface,' I muttered.

'Come here then, Jack!' Ellie put out her arms and I dropped him on to her tummy.

'Sing with me. Happy birthday to you!' she started singing, and Jack gave a chuckle.

I flopped on to my bed, glad she was around. Glad of the respite. It had its drawbacks, being a single mum – mostly because it meant there was only one of you. You had no one to offload on to.

Ellie was a help, though. She'd changed a lot. Eighteen months ago, when I'd first found out I was pregnant, she'd been ten and a prissy, miniature version of Mum, all shock and horror. Pregnant at fifteen! The earth is going to open up and swallow you whole! Now she was twelve, though, we got on OK. She was really grown-up for her age: as tall as me and (although it killed me to have to say it) prettier. I'd seen boys hanging around outside the flats for her already. Mum blamed the boys business on me, saying that Ellie had grown up too fast because of 'what's happened in this family'. Anything like that was my fault, although actually, I'd only ever had one boyfriend in my life – the boy who'd got me pregnant.

Luke was at university and lived in Sheffield now. About as far away from me as he could get. He'd remembered it was Jack's birthday, though – he'd sent a horrible fluffy green troll thing, and it was that which had been wrapped in the red wrapping paper. A note round the troll's neck had said, 'Happy Birthday from your daddy' and I'd removed this before Mum had seen it and started on about it ('Fine daddy he's turned out to be. Seen his son twice in a year. He needn't think he'll get away without giving you maintenance as soon as he's earning,' etc etc).

I let it all go over my head. I had to with Mum. If I reacted to everything she said I'd go mad. Besides, I never defended Luke because I'd long since stopped feeling anything for him. Any love business between us had finished before I'd even had the baby. He was a million miles away in Sheffield and could have been on the planet Zog for all I cared.

'What time's Mark coming?' Ellie asked, looking at

me from under her eyelashes. She was wearing electric blue mascara, I noticed.

'What d'you want to know for?'

Ellie sat Jack on her pillow and gave him a book to look at. He began to gnaw the corner of it. 'I was just asking . . .'

'He's not going to be interested in you!' I said. He wasn't even interested in *me*. 'He's ten years older than you are.'

'So?'

'Besides, he's our cousin.'

'So?' she said again. 'It doesn't stop me fancying him.'

Mark was, I have to say, extremely fit. I'd spent most of Jack's early weeks in a tizz about him – until I'd found out that he was actually related to us. My Auntie Lorna had had a baby when she was seventeen and had it adopted, and that baby had turned out to be Mark. To be quite honest, it wasn't so much finding out we were cousins that had stopped me fancying him, but realising that he wasn't the slightest bit interested in me.

I'd had a bit of a crisis then and it had made me stop and think: who *was* going to fancy me? Ever? A girl of sixteen with a baby in tow? The answer was, practically no one. And once I'd realised that it meant I could stop thinking that some gorgeous boyfriend was going to come round the corner at any minute. It just wasn't going to happen.

'I didn't fancy boys when I was your age,' I said to Ellie. 'I was into plastic ponies.' I glanced at Jack, who was still gnawing the book. It was blue, and there was a stream of blue dribble about to go on to his T-shirt. I pulled a tissue out of a box and caught the dribble just in time.

'I only want to look at him,' Ellie said. 'I'm not going to fling myself at him. Anyway, what time is his *mum* getting here?'

I grinned at the way she'd said it. Mark's mum – our Auntie Lorna – was my dad's younger sister, and when I was pregnant and excluded from school I'd been sent away to stay with her. It was only then I'd found out that, twenty years before, she'd had a baby of her own who'd been adopted.

I glanced at my watch. 'She's supposed to have been here by now. She wanted to arrive before the party started and before Mark arrived.'

Ellie gave me a wide-eyed and wondering look. 'How weird was that!' she said. 'I still can't believe he's our cousin. Fancy Auntie Lorna . . . How many times have they seen each other now?'

'About four, I think,' I said. 'Lorna wants to see him more, but he's being a bit offish. I don't think he's properly forgiven her for getting shot of him when he was born.'

'At least she *had* him,' Ellie pointed out. 'She needn't have done. She could have had an abortion or something.'

I nodded, watching Jack. He'd dropped the book and rolled himself on to his tummy, then wriggled and kicked until he was at the edge of the bed. He dangled his fat little legs until they reached down to the floor, then put his weight on them and stood for a moment, swaying, before he collapsed.

I clapped him. 'Clever Jack!'

'Just look!' Ellie said admiringly. 'It won't be long before he's walking.'

Jack shuffled forward on his bottom, then rolled sideways and went under the bed and straight into a wodge of fluff.

I groaned. Mum's predictions had an uncanny way of coming true – he *was* going to be filthy before we started the party. Grabbing him, I brushed down his T-shirt, and as I did so there was a ring at the doorbell.

'I'll go – in case it's Mark,' Ellie said, batting her blue eyelashes.

She went off and I looked at myself in the mirror. My hair was long and a bit straggly – I hadn't had it cut for ages because I couldn't take Jack in the hairdressers with me – and anyway, it cost too much. I hadn't bothered with any make-up either. I never did these days. I might wear a bit of lippy or something when I went to the educational unit in term-time, but when I was at home no one ever saw me except Jack, so it didn't seem worth the bother.

But now, seeing as it was a *party* . . .

I rummaged in a drawer for my make-up bag and found, among the broken eye pencils, sample sizes of moisturiser and grubby pieces of cotton wool, the remains of what had once been my favourite lipstick. That was another thing about being a teenage mum: no money. After buying Jack's nappies and jars of baby food and whatever shampoos and stuff he needed each week, there was never anything left over for me. The things I had in my bag were crumbling to bits and it was a lucky day for me if I found a magazine with a free mascara or something on it.

I dug my fingernail into the lipstick and rubbed

what I could get over my lips. Then I found Ellie's make-up, in a smart silver wire basket, and borrowed her eyeshadow. Bit of a role reversal, I thought – it was supposed to be her who was pinching mine.

I listened at the door to find out who'd arrived. It wasn't Mark, though, it was Claire, supposed best friend. And unfortunately, she had Josie with her.

They came steaming into the bedroom with screams of jollity.

'Where's the birthday boy, then?' Josie cried. I looked at her. She'd always been slim but now she was as thin as a whippet, with spiky hair which was half blonde and half dark. She had a tattoo of a bracelet around her upper arm and, though I could never decide if tattoos were naff or not, I had to say she really looked good.

'Can't wait to see him!' Claire said, which was a bit rich, I thought. If she really couldn't wait to see him, then why hadn't she been round here in five weeks? Claire was looking good, too: slim and nicely made-up, with shiny cheekbones and a really tight pair of leather jeans. Next to them I felt like Mrs Frump.

'There he is!' Josie swooped on him and picked him up. 'He's gorgeous! Hasn't he grown!'

As she hadn't seen him for about four months, I thought he probably had.

'He's lovely!' Claire said. 'And isn't he beginning to look like Luke?'

I nodded, mentally pricing up her jeans and her top. If I wanted them (and I'd have killed for them, actually) I would have to go without food for at least six months.

They both gave me presents for Jack. Claire's was a photo album with BABY in furry writing on the front, and Josie's was a plastic duck on wheels which pushed along with a loud *quack-quack-quack*.

They sat down on the bed while I showed the presents to Jack. Josie had him on her knee and was jogging him up and down enough to make him sick. He sat there, startled, staring at her while she jiggled and made kissing noises.

'Oh, isn't he gorgeous! Megan, you're so lucky!' she cooed. 'It's so cool to have a baby. Wish I had one!'

I didn't bother to say anything to such a blatant lie. If anyone wanted a baby that badly then they knew how to get one. They'd seen me, though. They'd seen boys shouting after me at school and seen me pushed away with Auntie Lorna in Cheshire to live for most of my pregnancy. They'd seen – and were still seeing – me miss out on parties and discos and boyfriends and holidays and about a million other things. Lucky? I didn't think so.

CHAPTER TWO

Lorna – I didn't call her Auntie any more – was sitting on the arm of the sofa, looking nervously along the hall towards the front door. The party was well under way. Mark had just arrived and at the end of the hall I could see Ellie, giggling and messing around with him, first of all pretending to shut the front door on him and then letting him through.

I wondered how Lorna felt. I couldn't imagine. For a start I couldn't think what it would be like to have Jack grown-up, as old as I was, a real person. And then neither could I think what it would be like if I'd given him up for adoption – even though when he was born I thought I might have to do that.

Jack, who was sitting on Claire's lap now, suddenly flung himself back and gave a tired-sounding cry, and I turned automatically to take him from her. I'd been desperately hoping that he wouldn't be fidgety and grizzly for the party, or insist on having his bye-byes to hold, be sick over anyone or scream at the top of his voice if I had to stop him from doing something. I wanted him to play Perfect Baby so that everyone would think how well I was managing. I never wanted anyone to feel sorry for me.

Jack suddenly saw Mark and cheered up. Just that week he'd started to point, and he did it now, giving excited squeals as he pointed down the hall.

As Mark came into the room with Ellie practically hanging off the hem of his jumper, Lorna gave him a quick, bright smile. She stood up and hugged him and he more or less hugged her back, but briefly and stiffly, letting go of her well before she let go of him.

'Where's that birthday boy, then!' he said, and Jack gave an excited shriek as Mark advanced towards him, arms outstretched. I sat Jack down on the floor and Mark crawled round him, being a tiger. That was what Jack was missing, I thought: someone being a tiger. He didn't even have a grandad around – my dad lived in Australia with his second family.

Mum came in from the kitchen. She said hello to Mark and frowned at Ellie, shaking her head slightly to try and stop her hanging round his neck. 'Now, what time shall we have tea?' she asked. As I opened my mouth to reply she added, 'As soon as possible, I should say. Before Jack gets irritable.'

'Tired,' I substituted.

That was another thing. It was all right if I thought he was grizzly and tiresome, but let Mum or anyone else try and infer it and I got furious. No one was allowed to criticise him but me – and then I only did it to myself.

Claire and Josie looked towards Mark and I could see them both adjusting themselves slightly, getting smilier, putting themselves at a better angle, tossing back their hair. Yeah, he was a good-looking guy all right.

'What did Luke send you?' Josie asked me.

'Have you heard much from him lately?' Claire added.

'I had a letter with his present,' I said. I picked up the horrible troll thing. 'This is it.'

They both pulled faces. 'I would have thought he'd have sent something nicer than that,' Josie said.

'Just shows,' Claire added.

Josie glanced at me. 'What time d'you think this will be over?' she asked. 'The party, I mean. Because Claire and I thought we'd go down to *California's* later.'

I stared at her. I didn't really want her here in the first place but – bloody cheek! – she was talking about going already. 'Don't you have to be eighteen to get in there?' I asked. I'd heard about *California's*: it was a trendy wine bar place, all frosted glass and pale wood, with guest DJs mixing.

Claire shook her head. 'We went last Saturday,' she said. 'As long as you get there before the bouncers arrive and don't make it obvious that you're drinking, it's OK.' She turned to Josie. 'But we're not going for ages yet, are we?'

'I was just asking,' Josie said.

I shrugged nonchalantly. 'Don't know what time it'll finish. Whenever. You don't have to stay any longer than you want to.' You can sod off now if you like, I thought.

'It's not that,' Claire said quickly. 'If you don't get in there early the bouncers will be there and they'll want ID.' She looked across at Mum. 'Why don't you come with us. Your mum'll babysit, won't she?'

I shook my head. 'That's OK,' I said. 'I'd better stay here tonight.' I could go out – I did sometimes, but not very often. Mum had this thing about me being responsible for Jack. There was a particular line of nagging which began, 'He's your baby. You wanted him and you've got to look after him.' This then progressed to, 'I've done all the looking after babies that

I'm going to do. Don't forget I was left with you and your sister to bring up single-handed.' And always finished up with, 'You've made your bed and you'll have to lie in it.'

'Anyway, I couldn't really go out on Jack's birthday,' I said to Claire now.

Josie smiled over at Mark and brushed a speck off her silk top. It was really expensive, I could see that from the cut of it and from the little designer logo. She stroked her bracelet tattoo, as if to draw attention to that and to her slim brown arms. I hoped and prayed Mark wouldn't fancy her – either of them, actually, but especially her.

'Megan!' Mum called from the kitchen. 'Can you give me a hand, please?' She was speaking in her posh voice but it had risen to dangerously high levels.

'Cut the crusts off those sandwiches!' she snapped when I got in there. 'Then stick that big blue candle on the birthday cake and find some serviettes in one of the drawers and put them out.' She sighed impatiently. 'I thought my days of children's birthday parties were over and done with but now I find I've got to do them all over again. See if that jelly's set, will you?'

'I didn't ask you to do a party. And no one will want jelly!'

'This is a baby's birthday party, Megan. People will expect jelly. You've got to do these things properly.'

That was it, you see. She always knew best. She was my mother and no matter that I was a mum myself now, she knew how to do things: feed babies, wind babies, change babies, talk to babies, buy things for babies, put babies to bed, get babies up, teach babies to speak/wave/sit/stand/walk. She knew everything and I didn't. This was all the more annoying because it was true.

As I searched for serviettes I heard a familiar whimper which turned almost immediately into a cry. Jack had become really clingy lately – that was another reason it was difficult to go out and leave him. He was OK while I was in the room, but immediately I disappeared he'd start.

I abandoned the search for the serviettes, stuck the candle on the cake and went towards the door. 'Don't just disappear – I want some help in here with this tea,' Mum said. 'I've told you before, you shouldn't go to him straightaway. If you do that he'll expect you to return and amuse him every time he cries.'

'I don't want him upset at his own birthday party!' I said.

'And I don't want to have to cope with all this on

my own – at my age I should be putting my feet up a bit, not running round after babies. Put the kettle on, get me a new packet of teabags out of the cupboard in the hall – and then find a small jug to put that cream in, will you?'

Yes, oh slave mistress, I thought.

'And don't go back to that baby for at least five minutes. You'll spoil him the way you're going on, you mark my words.'

No, in the circumstances, I wouldn't ask Mum if I could go out . . .

It was just as everyone was leaving that the phone call came. Lorna had gone earlier to get her train back home, and about six o'clock Mark said he had to go and do something in the office of the newspaper where he was a photographer. By sheer coincidence, Claire and Josie decided they wanted to leave then, too: I thought they'd probably walk up to the bus stop with him and then drop a big hint about going on to the wine bar, hoping that he might say he'd join them later.

Ellie went to answer the phone, called out that it was for Mum and then came to join me in the kitchen. Jack was in his baby chair chomping on his dummy and I was warming a jar of baby food in the microwave. His T-shirt was rainbow-coloured with the remnants of pink jelly, chocolate cake, iced buns and yellow egg mayonnaise but I wasn't sure if he'd eaten anything substantial enough to get him through the night. He only had a bottle of milk at night now and Mum always kept on about him getting enough vitamins and minerals and things.

'Who was that?' I asked Ellie, because Mum didn't exactly have a load of people ringing her, especially on a Saturday night.

'Dunno,' Ellie said. 'A man.'

We looked at each other, mystified.

'Must be someone selling something – double glazing,' I said.

'No, he asked for her by name. He said, "Can I speak to Christine?"'

'I hope he said, "Can I speak to Christine, *please*."' This was one of Mum's little rules. We both giggled and then I said, 'Perhaps she's got a boyfriend.'

'As if!'

I tipped Jack's food into a bowl, whipped out his dummy and put a spoonful of creamed chicken into his mouth. Because he wasn't really hungry he opened his mouth wide and the mixture ran out and straight down his plastic bib.

'She must have had someone since Dad, though,' I said. I put another mouthful in and this time a lot of it stayed there. Jack made chewing movements with his mouth. He couldn't actually chew anything properly because he didn't have back teeth, but he was trying.

Ellie shrugged. 'I can't remember anyone.'

'In twelve years, though!' I lowered my voice. 'I mean, she's not that bad.'

Jack stopped chewing, opened his mouth wide and removed something – a piece of potato. He looked at this and squished it between his fingers before rubbing it on his cheek.

Ellie shook her head. 'No, I just can't see her with a boyfriend. She's too . . . too something. Too grown-up. Too much of a mum.'

I pulled a face. I didn't *think* I was . . . but maybe *I* was too much of a mum as well. Maybe I'd never have a boyfriend again in my life.

I finished feeding Jack and was wearily wondering if I could possibly get away without giving him a bath that night, when Mum came back into the kitchen. She didn't look at either of us, just went straight to the sink and started washing up. Ellie and I rolled our eyes at each other and after a moment Mum said,

27

'What're you two looking at me like that for?'

'We just wondered who was on the phone,' I said.

'Nothing to do with you,' she said sharply.

'I was only asking!'

'We thought you'd got a boyfriend!' Ellie said, and burst out laughing.

'Oh, you did, did you?' Mum said. That was all she said, but it was the way she said it.

Ellie and I made incredulous faces at each other. 'I'm just going to give Jack a once-over with a flannel and put him to bed,' I said. 'He's really tired.'

Mum turned. 'You're not putting that baby to bed without a bath!'

'I'm really whacked,' I said. 'It won't hurt. I'll bath him in the morning.'

'He's *filthy*!' Mum said. 'And not only that, a bath will relax him.'

'It won't relax me, though.'

'We're not concerned with you, we're concerned with the baby. He should come first . . . it's what's best for him that's important.' She gathered strength. 'A baby isn't something you can pick up and put down when you want to, you know. A baby is for life.'

'I thought that was a puppy,' I said. But I went to run the bath. It was easier.

CHAPTER THREE

'Of course, in my days, girls didn't have babies before they were married,' the taxi driver said.

'Is that right?' I asked politely. Big deal, I thought.

'Or if they *did* have them, they had them adopted.'

I glowered at the back of his fat neck. It was a few weeks after Jack's birthday party and I was in the back of a taxi on my way to Poppies – the educational unit-with-a-nursery where I was taking my A Levels. All last term I'd had the same, nice, younger driver who'd made jokes with me and taken an interest in Jack. That morning, though, the first day of a new term, a different, older man had turned up to collect me.

'All these taxis going backwards and forwards must be costing the authorities a packet. How many girls are there in that place you go to?'

'Depends,' I said. 'Eight or nine. Sometimes more.'

'And they all have taxis twice a day?'

I said yes and he went on, 'I might be talking myself out of a job, but I can't see why you girls can't get there and back under your own steam.'

I didn't say anything. Next to me on the seat sat Jack, in his new little carry seat I'd bought with some money my dad had sent me for his birthday, and on the floor in front of us was a big rucksack full of the things he needed to get through the day: nappies, food, changes of clothes, piece of blanket, feeding cup, changing mat and washing stuff. Alongside the rucksack was a big bag of books for the exam subjects I was taking. Imagine taking all that lot on three buses . . .

'It must cost the government thousands having you lot driven around,' he continued.

I pretended to be busy with Jack.

'I suppose you've got a nice flat, have you?' he went on after a moment.

'No, I haven't.'

'Because that's what they do, innit? They get pregnant and they get themselves on the housing list, and then they get a flat. Two–three bedrooms! And then they let out the spare rooms to their friends and make a mint. Oh, I've heard all about them.'

I began to hum under my breath.

'It's always the same. Free handouts to anyone who wants them! Bet you get a nice little allowance each week, taxi rides anywhere you want, free nurseries . . . '

I could feel myself beginning to get really angry. 'I'm taking my A levels next year, ' I said, 'and then I'll be able to put my son in a nursery and get a decent job. I won't need any handouts then.'

'So you'll be out to work all day, will you? Who's going to look after your kid, then? That'll be the state again, will it?'

I gave up, leaned back in my seat and stared out of the window. Jack had gone to sleep. He was teething and had been up three times in the night – not for long, though, but long enough to lose his dummy and need a cuddle. And for long enough to wake me up properly, so that each time I'd spent an hour or so staring at the ceiling, trying to sort my life out, wondering just what it was that I wanted to do with it. Or – not what I wanted to do with it – what I possibly *could* do with it now that I had Jack.

The traffic was bad that morning. We stopped and started and jolted around, and I was feeling sick by the time we got to Poppies.

The driver pulled up with another big jolt, waking Jack. 'You're here,' he said, and he didn't help me out with Jack, as the other one had always done, but left me to manage bags, baby, chair and everything on my own.

'Thank you very much!' I said. 'Lovely journey,' I added sarcastically – but very quietly. I had to be careful in case I had him for the rest of the term. I put the rucksack on my back, Jack over my arm in the seat, and dragged along the bag of books with the other hand.

Vicki appeared at the office door with a big smile on her face. She was the manager of the place and she was lovely – all the staff were. There were usually four or five of them: half looked after the babies and half tutored the lessons. Girls came and went: there were usually a couple of pregnant ones or girls with brand new babies, but there were also girls with toddlers; children up to three.

Poppies was actually four Portakabins linked together. Each had two rooms, and together they made a small school unit with a nursery attached. We were in the grounds of a big comprehensive, Oakley, although we were completely separate from them and couldn't actually see the school building from where we were.

'Good summer?' Vicki said, and beamed at Jack. 'Hello, my favourite boy!' she said, and he gave a scream of delight. 'He's getting along well, Megan,' she said, opening the inner door for me. 'He's looking really grown-up.'

'He's a year and a month now,' I said proudly. 'He's taking a few steps on his own.'

'Any words?'

'A few,' I nodded. 'He says "bye-byes" and "g'bye" and "'lo",' I said. 'But sometimes he gets the goodbye and hello muddled up and says goodbye when you meet him.'

Vicki laughed. 'We'll have him saying lots of words by the end of term,' she said.

As I went in, another taxi drew up at the gate and Vicki waved to the girl inside – someone I didn't recognise – and went down to greet her. I carried on to the nursery to settle Jack, really pleased to be back. Here, I had something to do and girls to chat to. If Jack was getting on my nerves I could offload him, and if I was worried about anything I could ask the staff. They obviously knew better than I did, but, unlike Mum, they didn't ram it down your throat.

Our lessons weren't like they'd been at real school, either – not half so disciplined. They couldn't be really, because although the girls turned up most days, if their babies were ill, their taxis didn't arrive or they just didn't fancy it, they didn't bother to come in. And sometimes lessons were disrupted by the babies or, more excitingly – as had happened last term – by a girl going into labour. It was all much more laid-back than school: if it was a nice day your tutor might take you out somewhere, to see an interesting building or something, or lessons would be shelved because someone had turned up from the health service and wanted to talk to us about a baby's speech development or the like.

I said hello to Joy and Stacey, two girls who'd been there last term, and we chatted a bit about what we'd done in the summer. Stacey had just got engaged to her boyfriend and was wearing a blue sapphire ring, which she flashed in front of our eyes at every opportunity.

There was a girl I'd never seen before sitting by the window with a very small baby wrapped tightly in a shawl on her lap. She was my age, or a bit younger, had fair curly hair and was pale and quite thin considering it couldn't have been long since she'd had her baby. She had some funny old clothes on, like jumble sale stuff, but maybe that was because she couldn't get into anything of her own yet.

'You OK?' I asked, because she was looking anxious.

She nodded. 'First day nerves,' she said.

I grinned. 'It's not like school – you don't have to

worry. Everyone's really nice.'

She shot a nervous look around the room. 'My landlady said they watch you all the time and if you don't look after your baby properly they tell you off.'

'Rubbish,' I said. 'If you do something wrong they tell you how to do it.'

She smiled a little. 'That's OK then.' She looked at Jack. 'You've got a little boy, have you?'

I nodded. 'He's Jack and I'm Megan.'

'This is a girl and her name's Stella. That means star,' the girl said. 'My name's Kirsty.'

I told her Jack was just over a year old and she said Stella was only three weeks.

'Where d'you live?' I asked, and she named an area in the opposite direction to where I came from. 'I'm in a Bed and Breakfast place,' she said, and pulled a face. 'It's horrible.'

'Haven't you got any family? Why aren't you living with them?'

'My mum said I'd get a flat quicker if they made me homeless.' She rolled her eyes. 'I didn't really want to, but I went along with it.'

'Don't you and your mum get along, then?' I asked. I put Jack down on the floor and he leaned on the chair in front of him and reached towards Kirsty's baby, patting her foot. 'Didn't she want you at home?'

'We've never really got on well,' the girl said, 'and then she met this bloke and now she wants to have a baby of her own with him. She said there wouldn't be room for me anyway, and that I'd get a place of my own quicker if they turfed me out.' She hesitated. 'Is it really OK here?'

'Yeah, it's fine!'

'Guess anything's better than walking round the streets. It's what I do mostly – I'm not supposed to stay in the B and B place during the day.'

'Why not?' I asked, shocked.

'Stella's crying wakes people up. There's a couple of men who work shifts and they don't like it.'

I pulled a face. 'That's their hard luck, then.'

'And the landlady says it's regulations or something – everyone's got to be out of the house for a certain number of hours.'

'I should ask Vicki about that,' I said. 'She'll have a word with them.'

She shook her head quickly. 'No, it's OK. I don't want to cause any fuss. They might think I've been complaining and then they'll be horrible to me.'

'So what's your room like?'

'Grim.'

'So's mine – and I live at home!'

Jack let go of the chair he was holding on to and lurched towards the big dolls' house. He took about five steps on his own before he fell on to it. I called, 'Hurray!' and he turned to smile at me, well pleased with himself. 'He's just starting to walk properly,' I explained to Kirsty.

'I can't imagine Stella *walking*. I can't imagine her any older than she is now.'

I grinned. 'I used to say that, but the time goes really quickly.'

The nursery was beginning to fill up. Girls gave their babies a last-minute rusk, or changed their nappies, or wiped their faces before they started lessons.

'Is Jack's father still around?' Kirsty asked. 'Is he your boyfriend?'

'*Was* my boyfriend,' I said. 'He's hardly been in touch since. What about you?'

She shook her head ruefully. 'I met him on holiday. Haven't seen him since.'

'Didn't you write to him?'

''Course. The address he gave me was a false one.'

I tutted – but the thing about having a baby when you're fifteen or so is that everyone had some sort of hard-luck story to tell. At Poppies last term there was

Gilly who'd had a baby by her best friend's boyfriend, Sinna who hadn't told her mum until half an hour before she'd given birth, Hannah who'd had a dozen boyfriends and had absolutely no idea who the father was and Suzie who'd got pregnant by her stepfather.

The holiday romance one was a new one on me, though. 'What a pig,' I said.

'Yeah,' she nodded. 'I thought he was really nice, too. He said he loved me.'

'Were you gutted?'

'Pretty much.'

'What about writing to the hotel you stayed in? Or getting in touch with the holiday company or something?'

She shook her head. 'I thought of all that. I don't even know if his name's right, though. And what would be the point?'

'You might get some money from him.'

'Do you get money from your ex-boyfriend?'

I shook my head. 'He's at university.'

'Is he any support at all?'

'Yeah. He sends Jack horrible green troll things on his birthday.'

She laughed. 'There you are, then.'

At least, though, I knew who he was and if I was

ever really desperate he'd probably help me. And of course I still had the security of being at home with Mum, even if she did drive me round the bend most of the time.

Maria – one of the tutors – came in. She said hello to everyone and went round admiring the babies, then she asked everyone who was doing Geography to go with her. Three of us settled our babies – I tried to ignore Jack's woeful look at me as I said goodbye – and followed her into one of the study rooms. As I closed the door I heard the first wail of protest from Jack, then for the next half an hour I tried to get into the session and ignore Jack's plaintive cries coming through the thin walls. Just as I thought I couldn't stand it any longer and would have to go to him, one of the nursery nurses came in to get me.

'He's going through a clingy phase, isn't he? He just wants you, I'm afraid.' She smiled apologetically. 'D'you think you can come and see to him?'

For the rest of the day, then, I did little bits of Geography interspersed with sitting in the nursery with Jack – and hoped that the clingy phase didn't go on for too long . . .

CHAPTER FOUR

My taxi usually came to collect me at four o'clock in the afternoon, but as it hadn't arrived by four-fifteen I took Jack and all my bags and baggages to the gate to wait. In the front of Poppies was a small garden with a couple of plastic toddler toys, and I sat Jack on the grass next to them and went outside to lean on the fence. I was looking down the road and so I didn't see or hear the boy until he was almost up to me.

'Hi!' he said, making me jump.

I turned. He was about eighteen, good-looking, with a shaved head and dark eyes. 'Have you just come outside for some air?' he asked, grinning.

I nodded. 'I'm waiting for my taxi.'

'You go here, then, do you?' he gestured towards Poppies.

'Yeah. I'm doing A Levels.' I put this in so he'd know I wasn't a bimbo. 'Are you at Oaklands?'

'In the Sixth,' he said. He looked over at Jack, who

was trying to pull himself on to a green plastic wheelbarrow. 'Is he yours?'

I smiled across at Jack. 'Yes, he is.' After the mess I'd got into when I'd first met Mark – trying to pretend that I didn't have a baby – I'd made up my mind that no matter who asked, shop assistants, people in the street, potential boyfriends, I'd tell the truth. Besides, I was standing outside an educational unit for single mothers so it was a bit obvious. 'His name's Jack.' I looked at him again and laughed because he'd just pulled the little wheelbarrow on top of himself and had such a baffled, surprised look on his face.

'Cute!' the boy said. 'My name's Jon. J-O-N,' he spelled out. 'How old is he, then?'

'Just over a year.'

'Has he got any brothers and sisters?'

'No, he hasn't!'

'Just checking,' the boy said. 'You on your own, then?'

I looked at him indignantly. 'Bit nosy, aren't you? What's with all the questions?'

'Sorry,' he said, 'but you don't often get good-looking girls waiting around outside here. And I like to get my facts right before I start.' He looked at me with raised eyebrows, smiling slightly. His eyes were very deep brown and considering it was years since anyone had flirted with me, I couldn't help but smile back. Start *what*? I wanted to ask.

'I've been coming here for ages. Since January,' I said.

'Well, I certainly didn't spot you before.' He gave me a look again, as if to say that if he *had* spotted me he'd have made a move. 'I came by bike all last term – went round the main road way.' He looked at Jack again. 'So he's yours, is he? You're pretty young, aren't you?'

'So?' I said defensively.

'So nothing. I was just saying. What's it like having a baby to bring up?'

I opened my mouth but then realised there was nothing I could say to answer. How could I tell him what it was like? There was too much . . . too many things. They couldn't possibly be rolled into something flippant and tossed back. I hesitated. 'It's OK,' I said.

I looked at Jack. He was on his tummy and, looking intently at a clump of grass, was trying to put some into his mouth. I left the boy – Jon – went over to the fence and picked up Jack, then opened his mouth and pulled out a few strands of greenery. 'Grass isn't nice to eat,' I said, and he just looked at me unblinkingly. 'Grass,' I said again, and pointed to it. Vicki had told us today that we ought to do this all the time, that naming things would help our babies' vocabulary.

'Do you get out much, then?' the boy called.

Just in case I went red again, I kept turned away slightly so he wouldn't see my face. I didn't want him to think I was so much of a bozo that I couldn't chat to a boy without going all stupid. Anyway, what was going on? *Was* he chatting me up? Was asking me if I went out much a preliminary? And – given that he was obviously sharp, easy to talk to and had the most fantastically high cheekbones – what should I say next? Cool or keen? God, I'd been out of touch for so long that I'd forgotten the rules.

Before I could decide what to say, my taxi pulled up at the kerb with a squeal of brakes and the driver – this morning's driver – hooted at me. I opened the back door of the cab, lifted Jack in, and then turned to collect my other stuff.

Jon handed it in to me. 'See you again soon, Gorgeous!' he said.

'See you,' I echoed, and clambered into the cab all confused.

When I looked past the driver's fat neck I saw his

eyes in the mirror, looking at me knowingly. 'New boyfriend, eh?' he asked. 'Trying it on, was he?'

I gave him what I hoped was a withering expression and didn't reply.

Jack went to sleep on the way home. I tried to keep him awake, pointing at things out of the window and naming them until I was bored enough to scream, but in the end his little head lolled to one side, his lids fluttered down and, while I was holding him up and saying 'Car!' for the zillionth time, he went out for the count. I laid him on my lap, smoothed his dark hair and admired his long eyelashes. He looked lovely when he was asleep – but that was three sleeps he'd had today, which meant that it would be the devil's own job to get him off tonight. I yawned widely to myself at the thought.

'Hard work, is it?' the driver said sarcastically.

On our way home we passed my old school, the one I'd been excluded from when I'd been pregnant. I stared across the playground: I could see a couple sitting on a wall. Was one of them Claire? Who was she with?

If I hadn't got pregnant I'd be going there now and Claire and I would be doing our A Levels together.

I'd be part of the group she belonged to who had bar-becues and discos and trips away together, who went to pubs and *California's* and had Saturday jobs and bought clothes – even sometimes bought cars – and had a laugh. I wouldn't be tied down and lumbered.

I strained to see if it *was* Claire, but a stream of cars passed on the other side of the road and I wasn't sure. We went round the corner and I leaned back in my seat. How weird to think that one night and one moment had led to a complete and utter trans-formation of my life. I wasn't the same person any more.

When would the real me come back? Would she ever?

When I got home, Mum was already in – she worked in an estate agents and did funny hours – and was doing something busy at the kitchen sink. Ellie was writing in a school book at the table and she came and took Jack from me, whispering in my ear, 'Watch out – bad mood!'

Mum turned to look at me. 'I came home from work early and happened to go in your bedroom. I could hardly walk in there for mess. Ellie's things were all cleared away but I couldn't even *see* the carpet for your stuff!'

'Hello Megan. Hello Jack,' I said. 'Did you have a nice day?'

'Never mind that,' Mum said. 'What're you going to do about that room?'

'I can't do anything, can I?' I said. 'I can't tidy things up because there's nowhere to put them. It's not my fault if Jack's got so many toys and things.'

'You could keep things cleaner and tidier than they are,' she said, and I could see what sort of a mood she was in because she'd got all our mugs out of the cupboard and was scrubbing at their insides with a little brush. 'You could keep some semblance of order in there. As it is, it's complete chaos.'

Hearing his nan shouting, Jack's bottom lip began to tremble.

'You're making Jack cry,' I said.

'I'm not talking to you, precious,' she cooed to Jack. 'I'm talking to that naughty mummy of yours. What sort of an example is she setting you, eh? It's not very nice living in a pigsty, is it?'

The phone rang and Ellie and I looked at each other. 'I'll go!' we both said, just to get out of the room, but as Ellie was still holding Jack I got there first.

'May I speak to Christine?' a man's voice asked, and I was so surprised I think I might have gasped. A man again. The same one who'd rung at Jack's birthday party?

I played for time. 'I'll just see if she's in,' I said. 'Who's calling, please?'

'It's George,' the voice said. 'George Simpson.'

I stood there with the receiver pressed against my ear, listening hard, as if I could somehow absorb further information from down the line. I wanted to know more. If we were the sort of family – if Mum was the sort of woman – who had loads of friends and relations calling all the time it would be different and no big deal, but we didn't. So who *was* George Simpson? Did she work with him?

I put the receiver down on the hall table and went back to the kitchen. Mum was looking at me expectantly. 'It's for you,' I said, and she did no more than drop the scrubbing brush and dash off, still with wet hands, to answer it. She reached the phone and then came back to close the door firmly behind her so that we couldn't eavesdrop.

'Oooh!' I said to Ellie. 'That was a man again. George Simpson.'

Ellie looked mystified. 'Never heard of him.' She held Jack out at arm's length. 'This baby needs changing.'

'Hang on a sec,' I said. I tiptoed to the door and opened it a crack.

'I see. Of course. Yes, perhaps,' she was saying in a low voice.

'It's not double glazing,' I said to Ellie. 'It's not that sort of conversation.'

I listened again. 'Well, if you think so,' Mum said. 'Yes, I'm sorry too.'

'She's sorry about something!' I whispered to Ellie behind me.

I turned back to the door to hear more, but Mum looked across and saw me. 'Close that immediately and don't be so nosy!'

I sat down at the kitchen table, grinning at Ellie. 'It must be a man.'

'With the name George Simpson I expect it is,' Ellie said.

'You know what I mean. *A man*. A boyfriend.'

'D'you think so?' Ellie asked. 'Mmm,' she said thoughtfully. 'She's made a few phone calls in the evenings . . . and she's always made-up now when she goes to work.'

We could hear some more murmuring from the hall, then a moment or two later there came the sound of laughter. Our jaws dropped.

A moment later Mum came back into the kitchen.

'Just a friend, was it?' I said after she'd started hammering at the mugs again.

'Never you mind,' Mum said. 'That's for me to know and you to wonder.'

Ellie and I made faces at each other. At least she was in a better mood . . .

CHAPTER FIVE

My taxi driver was in full flow all the way home on Friday, but I just let him rant on. I was a bit miffed because, just as we'd driven away from the educational unit, I'd seen Jon jogging up the road and looking, it seemed to me, as if he was heading straight for Poppies. He must have been going to see me. I'd already seen him once in the week, but my driver had been early and we'd only had time to exchange a few remarks. He'd called me Gorgeous again, though, and said I had very kissable lips, and though I knew it was probably all baloney I didn't care. Now I'd missed him, though, and I had a whole weekend ahead with no hope of seeing him.

I turned to watch his progress up the road, pressing my nose against the glass, and the taxi driver saw me. 'That your boyfriend?' he said, and then added with satisfaction, 'Looks like you missed him.'

Well, if he was that keen, I thought, he'd turn up again. If he wasn't – well, I could handle it.

As the taxi pulled up outside the flats ('These council flats, are they? Suppose your rent's paid by the government. All right for some!'), Mrs Brewster was standing on the pavement. Mrs Brewster – Ellie and I called her Witch's Brew – was about eighty, lived in our block and took a keen interest in what was going on. She'd had a field day when she found out about Jack, but she wasn't an entirely horrible old bat because she'd actually knitted me quite a lot of things for him. They weren't Designer Baby but when you're on income support you can't care about that.

She waited while Jack and I emerged with all our stuff. 'How's this lovely lad?' she said, poking a bony finger under Jack's chin and tickling him.

'Bye!' Jack said, showing his two teeth.

'He's fine, thanks.' I shut the taxi door after us and Witch's Brew insisted on carrying Jack's changing mat and bag into the flats and up the stairs. 'Not wearing any of my woollies, then?'

'It's too warm at the moment,' I said. 'Soon as it gets cold, he'll have them on.'

We reached the top of the stairs; our flat was just along the corridor. I glanced down, saw two people standing outside it and tried to take evasive action.

'It's all right, thanks, Mrs Brewster. I'll take that mat now,' I said.

'No, no. Let me help you,' she said. She was insisting not because she really wanted to help, but because she'd seen what I'd seen: Ellie outside the door of our flat, locked in a clinch with some boy.

As we advanced on them I coughed loudly. They didn't move. I could hardly believe it. A week or so ago she'd been playing with dolls, now she was snogging! I knew for a fact I hadn't snogged anyone when I was only twelve.

I coughed again – right in her ear, practically – and they broke away. The boy, who was about the same age, looked embarrassed, but Ellie just smiled uncaringly. 'Hi!' she said. 'Hello, Mrs Brewster.'

I looked pointedly at the boy. 'Who's this, then?'

'This is Jamie.'

Jamie muttered something.

'Your boyfriend, is it?' Witch's Brew asked.

'Sort of.'

The old girl gave her a knowing look. 'You want to watch out. I don't want to be knitting another set of baby clothes for you, lass.'

I glowered at Ellie. 'Coming inside?' I asked pointedly.

'I was just saying goodbye to Jamie.'

'Bye!' Jack said, getting it right for once.

'I think you've already said it.' Bundling Ellie in, I left Witch's Brew to walk Jamie off the premises and discover what she could.

'You haven't let that boy come in here, have you?' I asked before we were even through the door.

'What if I have?' Ellie asked, wide-eyed. 'He's only a friend. He just came in for a cold drink.'

'Is that what you call it? Only a *friend*!' I said. 'I should hate to see what you'd get up to if he was your boyfriend.'

'Do leave off. You sound just like Mum.'

I put Jack down on the floor in the hall and he immediately pulled himself up using the legs of the hall table, and began to make his way unsteadily into the kitchen, holding on to the walls.

'Mum would go mad if she knew that boy had been in here,' I said.

Ellie just shrugged.

I heard a faint squeak as a kitchen door was opened. Then came the noise Jack made when he was greeting the saucepans. I looked at Ellie closely. 'You wouldn't, would you?'

'Wouldn't what?'

'Sleep with him.'

She gave a short scream. 'Of course I wouldn't. D'you think I'm mad?'

'Only . . .'

'You don't have to tell me anything,' she said. 'I've got no intention of sleeping with anyone yet. For years and years. Give me some credit!'

'Yes, well, that's what I said, and then things happened and everything got sidelined.'

'Apart from anything else, I think two babies in this flat might be a bit too much,' Ellie said.

There was a crash from the kitchen and I ran in to see Jack sitting on the floor surrounded by two colanders and an assortment of saucepan lids.

I looked round: the place was a mess. The worktops were covered in a sea of bottles, feeding cups, dishes, packets of this and that, things to be washed up and things washed but not put away. An enormous pile of washing was strewn in front of the machine and on the worktop sat a basket full of ironing. Mum had already had a fit about the state of things before she left for work and I'd said I'd tidy up, but I hadn't had time to do anything before I'd left.

'Look at this place!' I wailed.

'I've got to do my homework,' Ellie said.

'So have I.' I looked round again. 'Mum will go mad if she comes in and sees it like this.'

Ellie shrugged. 'What's new? She's always going mad.' Sticking her Walkman in her ears she went into our bedroom. I leaned over Jack, put the kettle on for a cup of tea and then noticed that the milk hadn't been put back in the fridge that morning. I sniffed it and realised it had gone off.

Jack saw me looking at the milk and stretched his arm up, making a noise that meant he wanted some.

'There isn't any,' I said, turning the kettle off. I sighed heavily. *Now* I'd have to go down to the corner shop and get some milk. Mum always liked a cup of tea as soon as she came in from work.

I picked up Jack and took him in to Ellie, who was sprawled on her bed reading a magazine. 'I thought you had homework to do.'

'This *is* homework.' She smiled at me sweetly. 'We've got to write a short story.'

'Look after him, can you? I've got to go down for milk.'

Jack lurched towards her, trying to grab the magazine with sticky fingers, and Ellie pulled a face. 'Do I have to? I can't do anything if he's around.'

'Join the club,' I said, shutting the door on them

both. I found a few coins in the bottom of my bag and went out. OK, maybe I wasn't being fair to Ellie, dumping Jack on her, but (as Mum never tired of telling us) life wasn't fair, was it? And she *was* his auntie. If I'd had to take him with me it would take ages just to get him and the buggy ready and the shop would probably be closed before we got there.

As soon as I was down those stairs and out of the flats I felt better. I was in the world again, normal, free of everyone: *child free*. I could be me for ten whole minutes.

I dawdled in the shop, spending a luxurious amount of time looking in the chill cabinet for the right sort of milk, then made the happy discovery that I had enough money left over for some sort of sweetie treat. I spent another few moments choosing chocolate buttons – normally I would whip past that counter in double-quick time before Jack saw what was on offer and starting wailing for something.

With three chocolate buttons placed along my tongue, I started back down the road. As I neared the flats, though, my feet began to drag. Everyone else in the world was looking forward to the weekend, but all the weekend meant to me was a trip into town to buy the biggest batch of disposable nappies for the smallest possible price.

A red BMW was parked outside our flats. I might not have noticed it except that when I got closer I saw that the registration number was LET 2, and wondered vaguely whose it was and why it had that on it.

I then noticed Mum was in the passenger seat.

I stopped, pretending to examine one of the dusty bushes on the pavement. What was she doing? We didn't have a car of our own and she always went to work by bus. Then I thought: LET 2 – *estate agents*! It had to be someone from work who'd given her a lift. Was this the man, then? Was this the mysterious George Simpson and his car?

I climbed over the low wall that led into the flats and walked up towards the fire escape. Mum – *with a boyfriend*. I just couldn't imagine it. But maybe it wasn't. Maybe it was just someone giving her a lift home from work.

Half-hidden behind the fire escape stairs, I watched their heads in the car. His was moving around a lot, as if he was talking animatedly. Then I saw that he was laughing, and so was Mum. After a moment his head tipped sideways towards hers, as if he was resting his cheek on her head.

I stared disbelievingly. It *wasn't* just a lift home; I could see that even from a distance. As I watched, their heads moved towards each other: they were talking quietly and intimately. Closer . . . closer . . . my eyes nearly popped out of my head . . . don't say they were going to kiss! I couldn't believe it. Mum and snogging – the two words just didn't go together. First Ellie, then her. Everyone in my family was snogging except me.

I didn't want to see any more. I nipped up the fire escape and into the flats, bursting in on Ellie and telling her what I'd seen.

'I don't believe it!' she said, and we ran into the kitchen to see if we could glimpse any bit of the car out of the window. 'Why doesn't she bring him in? Why hasn't she said anything to us about him?'

'Dunno,' I said. I shook my head wonderingly. 'Is it serious, d'you think?' I went back into our bedroom and grabbed Jack, who was quietly sorting out the contents of the wastepaper bin. I brought him into the kitchen and found him Josie's toy duck to play with. Jack beamed at me, pleased. The duck was a treat – I usually tried to hide it because its quacking drove me mad.

'Maybe it's just a casual date,' Ellie said.

'Mum – *snogging*,' I said. 'She wouldn't do that unless it was serious.' I flicked the switch on the kettle again for a cuppa and looked round the kitchen. It *was* a mess, but if I let Jack keep the duck and if Mum could just stay outside in that car for about another twenty minutes, I reckoned I could fix it.

She was half an hour, as it happened, and by this time the kitchen was reasonably clear, one load of washing was on and there were potatoes in their jackets ready to cook in the microwave.

I thought I'd say straightaway that I'd seen her. 'Nice car,' I said.

'What do you mean?'

'I saw you in that Beamer,' I said casually. 'Someone give you a lift home, did they?'

'What d'you mean, you saw me? Have you been spying on me?'

'Don't get paranoid,' I said. 'I was just coming back from the shop and I saw you sitting in there. I wondered who you were with, that was all.'

'None of your business,' she said, but then after a moment added, 'Well, I suppose I might as well tell you. It's a friend of mine from work. His name's George – George Simpson.'

'Oh,' I said. Ha! I thought. It *was* him. 'Is he nice, then?'

'Very nice indeed,' she said crisply. 'And that's all you need know about him.'

An hour later we'd eaten our potatoes, the place was looking like a rubbish dump again and Jack was sitting under the table wailing. I'd put him to bed once and he'd screamed and screamed as if he had a pain, so I'd had to get him up again. I'd tried to sit him in his high chair while we ate, but he'd cried so much that Mum had told me to get him out of it and let him do what he wanted for ten minutes, just so we could eat in comparative peace. Being under the table and playing with our shoes had amused him for two minutes, then I'd got the quacking duck out again which had given us another couple of minutes, but now he was full-on wailing, tired and miserable, rubbing his face with his blanket.

I looked at him. His face was red and the whole of the front of his sleeping suit was wet with dribble, which meant he was teething. The health visitor had told me he was probably going to cut several teeth at once and I should be prepared for some disturbed nights.

Mum cleared her plate and got up. 'I'm going out

tonight,' she announced. 'So I'm going to put the water on and have a bath.'

Ellie and I looked at her in astonishment.

'Mum! Have you got a date?' Ellie asked.

'Is it George Simpson?'

'Don't look so surprised,' she said to us. 'I'm not completely over the hill, you know. People of my age are allowed to go out on dates.'

'Where you going?' I asked.

'Just out in the country for a drive and a drink,' she said. 'Can you clear up in here, Ellie?'

'I'm going out too!' Ellie said. I shot a look at her – not with that boy again, surely. She knew exactly what the look meant. 'I'm only going over to Neema's to watch a video,' she added.

'That's not fair!' I said immediately. 'I've already cleared up once today.'

Mum got up. 'I don't care who does it. Sort it out between you,' she said, going into the bathroom.

'I'll do it tomorrow!' Ellie disappeared into our bedroom at the speed of light and seconds – *seconds* – later I heard a carefree 'Bye, everyone!' and the front door close behind her.

There was a moment's silence while I looked at the amount of washing-up I had to do, and then Jack started wailing again. A sort of tired and moany wail that, I knew from bitter experience, could go on for hours.

Friday night, I thought. The weekend starts here. Yippee.

CHAPTER SIX

It was Sunday evening, Jack was in bed, Mum and Ellie were both out again and I was bored.

Yawning heavily, I flicked from channel to channel on the TV. Nothing! I had homework to do but I'd started reading it – 'The Love Song of J. Alfred Prufrock' by T. S. Eliot – and couldn't work out what was going on. What did it all mean? It didn't seem much of a love poem to me. And apart from old Prufrock I had washing, cleaning, ironing and wash-ing-up to do and I didn't feel like doing them, either. OK, at least Mum was out with George Simpson and so off my case, but with Ellie out as well it was deadly dull. There was no one to talk to – no one, even, to moan with about the stuff on the telly. It was all very well Ellie growing up and Mum going off and having a life of her own, but it didn't seem fair that they both had to do it at the same time.

I wondered if it had been like this for Mum after Dad had left. Ellie had been a baby, then, and I'd been about five, so until she'd started work she'd had no one grown-up to talk to for years and years. And no social life to speak of either – not until now, when this George person had turned up. But that, said a little voice inside me, was what happened when you had children. You had to put them first; make *them* your life. Everyone said so.

Sometimes, though, it didn't seem enough. Sometimes? Mostly.

I flopped down on the sofa and stared across at the horrible yellow-gold curtains, which had been hanging there ever since I could remember. The flat was not only a mess, it was a dump. We hadn't had any new furniture or carpets or anything for years.

I tried to buck up. OK, I had a spare evening, what could I do with myself? All the magazines tell you that an evening in on your own is something special, a treat. You're supposed to have a manicure and pedicure, then put bits of cucumber on your eyelids and have a face pack, then relax in a bubble bath with scented candles. I had no money for things like face packs or nail varnish or foot lotion, though, and anyway, the bathroom had peeling wallpaper and was crammed with plastic toys and baby stuff. If I wanted a bubble bath I'd have to use washing-up liquid, and there certainly weren't any scented candles around. That was *that*, then.

I closed my eyes. What would I like to be doing tonight? The answer was, I'd like to be going out somewhere for a meal, with someone I really fancied. Jon? Yes, Jon would do. I could quite easily work myself up into a Class A fancy for him. And if I wasn't with Jon, I'd like to be going out to a club. Or to *California's*, with Claire and without Josie. Or a disco where I could spend the entire night dancing – I couldn't remember the last time I'd been out dancing. I'd like to go out without having to leave bottles of milk and teething stuff and careful instructions about the bye-byes blanket, and without having to get back at a certain time.

I flicked through the TV channels again. 'Antiques Roadshow' was on. *Still*. It had been on for hours. All day, it seemed. I switched the set off and as I did so I heard a wail from the bedroom. I glanced at my watch disbelievingly: he'd only been in bed forty-five minutes! He'd been in a bad mood all afternoon, rubbing at his cheeks and dribbling, and though I'd been dying to get him to bed, I'd hung it out as long as possible hoping that he'd sleep right through the night. Forty-five minutes! How could he only sleep that long when he'd been so tired?

I turned the TV back on, found a wildlife programme and turned the sound right up. Every time there was a pause, though, I could hear Jack crying in the background. I left him about fifteen minutes, until I knew from the rattling of the bars of his cot that he'd pulled himself out of the bedclothes and was standing up.

I opened the bedroom door a tiny bit. If he didn't look too distressed then I'd leave him to it. He saw me first, though.

'G'bye,' he said in a little quavery voice and I immediately felt *terrible*. I picked him up and hugged him, and found he was damp right through his night-time nappy and sleep suit, and the bottom sheet was soaked. Sighing, I tugged at the sheet to pull it out and put in the wash. Ellie had got him ready for bed and she'd obviously done up the nappy wrongly. If you didn't get them just right then they leaked.

I changed him and took him into the sitting room. His tears had dried by now, there was just the occasional shuddering intake of breath to remind me that I'd been a cruel mummy and left him to cry. Immediately cheered up at the sight of his toys, he found Josie's duck and began to push it at speed up and down the room – *quack-quack-quack-quack*.

I let him play for ten minutes or so, and then tried to take him back into the bedroom. Realising he was about to be banished, he started crying as soon as I picked him up. I carried him in, though, arranged all his toys and his piece of blanket around him and said, 'Time to sleep. Night night!' very firmly. This is what the health visitor had instructed. Of course, he was roaring before I'd even closed the door.

I went into the sitting room and, to occupy myself, rang Claire. To my surprise, she was in – although she didn't exactly sound thrilled to hear from me. 'April brought over *Men in Black*,' she said. 'We were just about to start watching it.'

'Oh,' I said. 'Who's April?'

'She's a girl in my tutor group at school,' Claire explained. 'She's really nice. She's got the most fantastic red hair right down her back!' Then she said, 'Oh dear, can I hear someone crying?'

'Yeah,' I said. 'Guess who?'

'Aaahh,' she said insincerely. 'Sweet!'

'I'm about to chuck him out of the window, actually,' I said. 'I've had just about enough of him.'

There was a pause. 'Aaahh,' she said again, obviously not knowing what else to say.

In her background I could hear someone – the fantastically red-haired April, I supposed – saying, 'Who's that? Come *on*, Claire!'

'You'd better go,' I said. 'Your friend wants you.' You're supposed to be my best friend, I thought. Why can't you drop everything – drop April – and come over and cheer me up? 'Bye,' I said coldly. 'See you.'

She might have detected the icy tone in my voice.

'Megan – can't you get someone to babysit for you?' she said. 'You could come over here and watch the video with us.'

'Can't,' I said. 'Mum's out and Ellie's out.'

'Well, couldn't you pop over anyway?' she asked. 'Why don't you get Jack off to sleep and then come round. If I know you're coming we won't start the film till you get here.'

I was tempted. Claire's flat was only a block away. I calculated in my head: two minutes to get down our stairs, two minutes along the road, two minutes up her stairs. If I ran I could probably do it in five altogether.

'Go on,' Claire said. 'You'll like April. She's a laugh.'

'Well . . . ' I said. If I gave Jack another bottle it would send him to sleep, and then I'd have at least an hour before he woke up again. 'I don't know,' I said uncertainly.

'He'll be all right!' Claire said. 'If he's in his cot what can happen to him?'

Although I'd been thinking that myself, when she said it I immediately took the opposite stand. 'Loads!' I said. 'Suppose someone breaks into the flat? Suppose he climbs out of the cot? Suppose there's a fire? Suppose he coughs or chokes on his own sick?'

'Please!' she said, giggling. 'We've just eaten.'

'No, I'd better not,' I said.

'We've got popcorn!' she said persuasively.

'No, it's OK. Perhaps I'll see you in the week instead.'

'Yeah. Sure. Come round!' she said. 'My mum would like to see Jack.' I waited for her to say a day, or a time, but she didn't. Funny that, because when I'd been pregnant she'd promised that having a baby wouldn't change things between us, that we'd still be best friends, *always* be best friends. She was going to be Jack's fairy godmother, she'd said.

The April person yelled out again so we said goodbye. I put the phone down and heaved a big noisy sigh, feeling sorry for myself. It wouldn't have been too bad if I lived near any of the girls at the unit and could get to see them. Kirsty, for instance – I liked her best because she was sweet and not hard-bitten like some of the girls there. Also, when I heard her tales of the B and B it made me feel my own life wasn't too bad. I knew she'd love to get out of her horrible lodgings for an evening and come over, but she lived about twenty miles away, there was no proper bus route and she'd never have been able to afford a taxi.

Jack was still crying, of course, so I put one of Ellie's CDs on loudly to try and drown the sounds. After a moment there came a banging from down-stairs: it was Witch's Brew, who was immediately below us, thumping on the ceiling to protest at the noise. I turned the music down a little and could immediately hear Jack again, roaring louder than ever.

I'd go into the kitchen and wash up, I decided. Maybe I wouldn't be able to hear him from there. I'd leave him another fifteen minutes, and if he wasn't asleep by then I'd have to go and get him. If he worked himself up into a real lather he'd *never* sleep.

As I went into the kitchen the front door bell went. 'I've turned it down!' I shouted, thinking it was Witch's Brew coming upstairs to complain in person.

There was another knock. 'It's me. Mark!'

A visitor. Brilliant! I thought, running to the door to let him in.

'I can hear Jack crying right down the hallway,' Mark said, ruffling my hair. He was wearing a pale green shirt and a very soft black leather jacket and looked really good. When Ellie got home and realised he'd been, she'd probably slit her throat.

'Yeah. It's tough love time,' I said. 'I've got to get him trained properly. He'll be up all night every night otherwise.'

'But now his Uncle Mark's arrived . . . ' Mark said.

I grinned. 'OK,' I said. 'Go and get him.'

I started making a coffee and a couple of minutes later Mark was back with Jack, who was snuffling and rubbing his cheek with his blanket.

'I shouldn't let him get up again, really,' I said, 'but he hardly sees any men and I think he ought to.'

'That's right,' Mark said. 'You should always have your full quota of men.'

'Chance would be a fine thing,' I said, pouring hot water into mugs.

'No romance in your life?'

I shook my head. 'How about you?'

'Not bad,' he said. 'Couple of possibilities on the go.'

He sat down, still holding Jack, who for once wasn't struggling to rush away and play. Eyes closed, Jack had his head against Mark's and was rubbing Mark's cheek as well as his own with the blanket.

'He looks really sweet,' I said, almost forgetting that he'd been such a little beast. 'I wish . . . ' I hesitated. I'd been about to say I wished his own dad would take more of an interest in him instead of just sending trolls. I didn't just want a dad for Jack, though, I wanted someone who wanted me as well. 'There's this boy I've met and chatted to once or twice,' I said to Mark. 'He seems really nice.'

'Does he know about Jack?'

''Course!' I said. 'He's met him. He – this boy, Jon – is in the Sixth form near Poppies. I think . . . *think* he might ask me out.'

Mark raised his eyebrows. 'Hmm,' he said.

'What's wrong with that?'

'Nothing,' Mark said. 'Except I hope you're not thinking that he might be a permanent fixture in your life.'

'Don't be daft,' I said. But I was, of course. I couldn't help it. I'd been thinking about Jon asking me out and us getting on really well, and then him taking an interest in Jack and maybe, just maybe . . .

Well, as I'd said to Kirsty, it made a change from thinking about the price of disposable nappies.

Mark looked at me and shook his head. 'Forget it,' he said.

'What?'

'You don't really know him, do you?'

'No, but . . .'

'Take it from me, Megan, a boy of – what is he, seventeen?'

I nodded. 'I suppose so.'

'A boy of seventeen – all he's interested in is sex. He'll just be wanting a quick one and away.'

'How d'you know?'

'I've been there,' he said. 'No guy of seventeen is going to be interested in taking on someone else's baby. A ready-made family to provide for? Do leave off!'

'So you're saying I'll never get anyone!'

'No, I'm not,' he said. 'I'm just telling you that you won't get anyone your own age. Not at the moment. No one permanent.'

'OK,' I said, shrugging. 'I'll just go out with this Jon for a couple of dates, then. If he asks. It'll be better than nothing.'

'That's up to you,' Mark said. 'But don't get involved. You'll only get hurt.'

While Mark drank his coffee, Jack closed his eyes and his head dropped on to Mark's arm. I chatted to Mark about various things; about Mum and the mysterious George, and then I tried to think of a way of bringing the subject round to Lorna. Just as I was working out what to say, though, he looked at his watch.

'Got to split,' he said. 'I'm going to a flat-warming.'

'Can I come?' I asked wistfully.

'Got a babysitter?'

I shook my head. 'I'm only kidding. I haven't got anything to wear and my hair's hanging in grease – no one would let me into a party. Tell you what, though,' I went on, 'can you put Jack back to bed before you go? With a bit of luck he'll be off for good now.'

Carefully, without putting on the light, we tiptoed into the bedroom. I tidied Jack's bed and we laid him in it, with the special arrangement of bunnies, blanket and teddy that he liked. Then we covered him up and tiptoed out.

We went into the hall and as I opened the door for Mark, Ellie appeared with her hair done in little plaits with coloured beads on the ends.

'Well, look at you, Miss Ellie!' Mark said

admiringly, sending her into full giggle mode. All flustered and daft, she pleaded with him to stay. When he said he couldn't, she asked if she could go to the flat-warming with him.

'No, you can't!' I said, hauling her in. 'If I can't go, neither can you.'

Mark went off, and as I closed the door quietly and went down the hall holding my breath, I heard it: Jack's familiar starting-up cry, '*Wah-wah-wah wah*!' Each *wah*! louder than the one before.

'Brilliant,' I muttered to Ellie. 'The end of a perfect day and the start of a perfect night.'

CHAPTER SEVEN

I hated my taxi driver. He was a slimy creep, either wanting to talk about boyfriends or carrying on as if I was personally responsible for what he called the 'moral decline' in the country. Almost worse than this, he seemed to take a special delight in turning up just when Jon appeared in the road, or about half a minute after he'd arrived. Whenever he did this he'd say something like, 'Ooh, spoilt your fun, have I?' and smirk to himself. I had to put up with him, though. He'd been booked by the local authority for the whole term – maybe longer – and there was no way of getting to Poppies without him.

I thought a lot about what Mark had said about Jon only being after one thing and I decided that it very well might be true, but I wouldn't mind finding it out for myself. My reasoning was that all boys tried it on, and if I turned down dates just because of that then I'd more than likely go through the rest of my life without having any.

The following Friday morning, just when I was looking forward to another scintillating weekend, Kirsty arrived at the unit in a bit of a mess. I was in the little study re-reading *Wuthering Heights* before my tutor arrived and trying to work out whether Heathcliff was untamed and passionate or just spiteful and wicked, when a taxi pulled up outside and Kirsty got out, looking as if she'd come straight from bed in the clothes she stood up in. A screaming Stella was clutched in one arm and in the other she held an assortment of things: nappies, bottle, scarf, book, bag – one of which she dropped at every step.

I went into the hall. 'What's up?'

She looked desperate. 'I'm being chucked out of my lodgings!' she said, and burst into tears.

'Why?' I looked at her, amazed. 'They can't do that!'

'They say they've got to refurbish the rooms but I know it's because Stella's not going through the night yet. They hate me there. They're always complaining.'

Stella screamed on. Kirsty put the baby over her shoulder and put her own cheek down on to her head.

'I don't know what to do . . . '

I looked at Stella's little red screwed-up face.

'Is she crying now because she's hungry?'

Kirsty nodded. 'I couldn't get into the kitchen to warm her milk. And then when I did I found that someone had pinched all her bottles out of the fridge.' She looked at me desperately. 'I didn't have any sterile bottles so all she's had is boiled water.'

'Go and get a bottle from Vicki,' I said. 'She's got some formula milk.' I took Stella from her. The baby didn't look all that brilliant, actually – she had dried dribble all round her mouth and one of her eyes was sticky.

'I couldn't get in the bathroom, either,' Kirsty said, seeing me looking at her. 'So she hasn't been washed. They're doing it deliberately. They want me out!'

'Can't you speak to your social worker?'

She shook her head. 'I've tried to but she just says I've made myself homeless and if I can't cope then I should go back home.' Tears dripped down her cheeks. 'I can't, though. My mum doesn't want me . . . '

'Why don't you tell your social worker that?'

'I daren't!' Kirsty's eyes widened. 'They'll know we've been trying to beat the system. My mum said I've just got to sit it out no matter what. That they'll have to give me a flat in the end.'

I patted her shoulder, not knowing what to say. If

I'd had a flat of my own, I thought, then she could have come and stayed with me. For one wild moment I even thought about asking her to come anyway – and then I thought of the state of the place with the four of us all under each other's feet and didn't.

'Go and get a bottle for Stella,' I said. 'And then go and speak to Vicki about it. She'll be able to help.'

My tutor didn't actually turn up to do *Wuthering Heights* with me because she had another class, in another town, doing a test, so I shelved the Heathcliff question until later. I was left to my own devices quite a lot there, actually – I was the only one taking A Level English Lit and half the time I just had to get on with it on my own. Today this meant that I could help Kirsty out, though, and because she was really scared about telling Vicki I went with her.

It all got a bit serious then. Vicki said they had to consider Stella's welfare first, and that if Kirsty was being made homeless by her B and B then she might lose the right to come to Poppies, because her place was being funded by the specific area she lived in. If she wasn't living in that area there would be no taxis and no funding.

Kirsty just sat there crying, hunched over in the

chair with her arms around herself, rocking. I knew she mainly came to Poppies just to have something to do during the day, somewhere to go, not because she particularly wanted to take exams.

'Are you sure you can't go home?' Vicki asked. She sighed and looked at some papers. 'But even then you'd be out of our area.'

'My mum won't let me,' Kirsty muttered between sniffs and sobs. 'She doesn't want me at home all the time. And her boyfriend doesn't like Stella!'

'But maybe your mum could speak to him. Your home really is the best place for you, you know.'

Kirsty shook her head violently. 'I told you – my mum doesn't want me there!'

Vicki looked down at Stella who was asleep in one of the unit's carrycots next to her desk. 'Your baby doesn't look all that well-nourished at the moment, Kirsty.'

She didn't – even I could see that. Apart from the general grubbiness, she was so tiny and pale. But then Kirsty was quite tiny and pale, too. And sad-looking in her jumble sale clothes. I'd thought I was hard up, but Kirsty seemed even worse off than me.

'She's back to her birth weight!' Kirsty said defensively.

'She should be more than that now. What is she – five weeks old?'

'Six,' Kirsty said.

'Are you getting her weighed regularly?'

'Yes – here,' Kirsty said.

Vicki looked down again, tapping her pen on some papers. 'I'm afraid this is quite serious, Kirsty. I'm terribly sorry about your predicament but I'm going to have to let the social workers know about you and Stella. If your landlady chucks you out or makes it impossible for you to live there – well, we can't have you wandering the streets, homeless. Not with a baby.'

'But what will the social workers do? Will they get me a flat?'

'What they'll do is assess Stella, and assess you, to make sure you're both getting the care you need.'

'What does that mean?' I asked. 'Will they find Kirsty and Stella somewhere else to live? Will it be a flat or another Bed and Breakfast place?'

'Well, first of all they'll need to make sure that the sort of accommodation offered in lodgings is suitable for such an inexperienced mum with such a tiny baby,' Vicki said. She hesitated. 'It could be that they'll decide that Stella would be better off being fostered for a while.'

Kirsty started crying again.

'Just until you've sorted yourself out a bit,' Vicki went on, putting her hand on Kirsty's arm. 'Their priority is your baby. If they feel that Stella's failing to thrive – which means not getting on as well as she should – then they'll take steps to put that right. If those steps mean putting Stella with a foster mum for a few weeks, then that's what they'll do. And in the meantime they'll be looking for a proper home for you both.'

'I haven't been told that I've got to leave the B and B yet, though!' Kirsty said. 'They've given me four weeks' notice.'

'But if they're making things difficult for you, if you can't get in the kitchen to make your baby's bottles . . .'

'I'll speak to them!' Kirsty said desperately. 'I'll speak to the landlady and tell her what's happening. I'll say I'm getting another place soon.'

'From the sound of her, I don't think that will do much good,' Vicki said gently. 'But try, though. And if you give me the number I'll ring, too. We'll see what we can get sorted out over the weekend.'

'They won't take Stella away, will they?' Kirsty asked desperately.

'Well, we'll hope it won't come to that,' Vicki said. 'One more thing – have a think about any other places you could stay. Maybe you've got an older sister or aunt or someone you could live with?'

'No, I haven't!' Kirsty shook her head and started crying again.

Vicki said she'd keep Stella in there while she was asleep, so Kirsty and I went into the study room, where Kirsty collapsed in a heap.

'I know they're going to take her away!' she sobbed. 'I know they won't let me keep her.'

'They haven't said that,' I said. I thought about Jack and shivered. Although I complained about him, it would be unthinkable not to have him now. If anyone ever wanted to take him away . . .

'Look,' I said after few moments. 'You'll have to sort yourself out a bit. If Vicki comes along in a minute and you're still falling about the place crying then it's not going to look good. You've got to prove to her and everyone else that you can cope with things.

Kirsty thought about this for a moment, then nodded. 'OK,' she sniffed.

'I'm not being funny but why don't you go and tidy yourself up a bit?' It felt a bit mad to be telling someone else to do this, seeing as how half the time I went round looking like a dustbin. 'Wash your face and brush your hair and I bet you'll feel better.'

She did that – and did look better – and that afternoon Vicki got some sort of emergency fund money so that she could go out and buy six feeding bottles, a sterilising unit and a big packet of formula milk to replace the stuff she'd had pinched. They were both going to see what they could come up with over the weekend – and Kirsty also had to go round and ask her mum if she'd be willing to let her come home for a while.

Jon came along when I was hanging around for my taxi that afternoon. He looked really good – he was quite brown and his almost-shaved head was tanned, too. Jack was sitting quite happily in the little plastic truck in the front garden, so I opened the gate and went out into the road.

'Caught you!' Jon said. 'I've been along a couple of afternoons but I must have missed you.'

I smiled, pleased to see him. I still felt bad about Kirsty, though, so it probably wasn't much of a smile because he asked me what was up.

I shook my head. 'Nothing. It's just about a

friend of mine. How are you, anyway?'

'All the better for seeing you. Anyone tell you you've got lovely eyes?'

'What a line,' I said, though I was dead pleased.

'So where d'you live, then?'

I told him and he puffed out his cheeks. 'Blimey. I don't know how I'd get over there.'

So you *are* thinking about it, I thought. 'It's difficult without a car,' I said casually.

'And even if I got trains or something, how would I get home?' He looked me straight in the eye and added, 'Unless I stayed the night, of course.'

I felt myself going red and was quite relieved when my taxi squealed round the corner. 'Bit ahead of yourself, aren't you?' I said.

'Yeah. Maybe.' And then his eyes lit up and he smiled a really sexy smile. 'Doesn't hurt to ask though, does it?'

My taxi driver dropped me off outside my flats as usual later that afternoon ('You mind what you get up to at the weekend with those boyfriends of yours!') and with Jack slung round my hip, I climbed the stairs up to our flat. Another weekend with sod all to do. Something to dream about, though: Jon and what he'd said. It made me feel all funny just thinking about it . . .

Witch's Brew was just coming down the stairs. 'Lots going on in your flat today,' she said, patting Jack on the head.

Oh-oh, I thought: Ellie on the doorstep snogging again.

'People coming . . . people going,' she went on.

'What d'you mean? Who's coming and going?'

But she was trotting along the walkway to her own flat. 'You'll find out,' she said.

I watched her disappear, wondering what she was going on about. Maybe Ellie had asked loads of kids from school along for a video or something. Well, if she had they could all go home again.

I walked along to the flat. There was no noisy chatter, though, no loud music. Opening the door, I saw that Ellie's jacket and bag weren't there, so she wasn't even home.

Maybe old Witch's Brew was going a bit batty, I thought, and then I heard Mum's voice from the bedroom. 'No, over here!' she was saying, and laughing.

I just opened my mouth to bellow 'Mum!' and ask her what she was doing home, when I heard a man's voice.

'Really!' he said. 'At your age!' and then there was more laughter.

'Lo!' Jack called, hearing his gran. I just stood there, mouth open and gawping. Mum and a man. *In her bedroom.* What was going on?

CHAPTER EIGHT

I stood there for a moment, wondering what to do. Then I put down Jack and everything else and went back to open and close the front door again loudly so they'd know someone was home. Jack, seizing his opportunity, staggered into the kitchen and went straight for his favourite cupboard. *Crash!* I heard, as something hit the floor.

From the bedroom, Mum called, 'Is that you, Megan?'

'Yes!' I called back.

I heard the murmur of voices, and then a man said, 'Well, the sooner she gets used to it, the better.'

A tingle ran down my back. I didn't like the sound of that.

The bedroom opened and Mum appeared. She didn't look as if she'd just got out of bed or anything – she always looked neat and tidy whatever the occasion – but she did look a bit pink. 'Everything all right?' she asked me.

'Fine,' I said, and then I just looked at her, waiting. Past her, reflected in the mirror on her dressing table, I could see a man wearing a dark suit.

'Well, if your mother's not going to introduce me, I'd better do it myself!' a jovial voice said. The door opened wider and he stepped forward. He was short and quite squatty, with hair combed over a bald patch and a pale, freckled complexion. 'I'm George,' he said. 'George Simpson. I daresay your mum's told you about me.'

I shook my head slowly. 'No. No, she hasn't.'

'There hasn't really been the time, George,' Mum said, smiling up at him. 'And we didn't know events would overtake us quite so quickly, did we?'

'Indeed not,' George said.

'We knew Mum had a . . . ' I didn't really know what to call him. 'A boyfriend,' I said, for want of anything better.

'Ah, I think I'm a little more than that,' he said.

Yeah, I could see that, I thought – seeing as you were coming out of the bedroom.

'What George means is – he and I are engaged,' Mum said all of a rush.

I stared at her. 'What? How can you be?'

She laughed. 'Quite easily.' She held up her hand, 'See – engagement ring.'

I glanced at it, not knowing what to say. People their age getting engaged seemed bizarre. I knew people still did it – but young people, not your mum. And especially not to someone you didn't know. This George might as well be a stranger off the street for all I knew about him.

'Oh. Isn't it all a bit quick?' I said.

Mum smiled. 'George and I have been seeing each other for a few months now. And I've known him for years at work, of course.'

'That was before love blossomed!' George put in, giving her a hug, and I was practically sick on the spot.

Just as I was wondering what it all meant – I mean, were they getting married or anything? – Jack came into the hall with a colander in his hand. 'Bye!' he said to Mum, beaming at her.

'There's my boy!' Mum said, swooping on him and picking him up. Then she looked at him closely and said, 'Whatever has he been doing, Megan? He's absolutely filthy!'

'They had the sand tray out today,' I said, still thinking *what's this George doing here?* 'Jack wasn't allowed near it but two of the older kids gave him some sand to play with.'

'It's in his hair, nails . . . even in the crease of his neck!' Mum said, examining him all over. 'And he's got yellow stains all over his T-shirt. The babies should be more closely supervised, Megan. He could have eaten that sand!'

'He probably did,' I said.

Jack was staring at George, eyes wide.

'This is Jack. So what do you think of my grandson?' Mum asked George.

'Very nice, very nice,' George said smoothly, and I thought, I bet *he* hasn't had children. 'How old did you say he was?'

'Nearly fourteen months,' I said. I took Jack from Mum. 'So . . . now that you're engaged – what's that mean, exactly?'

'Well,' Mum said slowly, 'we're not only a proper couple, but George has come to live here with me. With us.'

'Oh.' I stared at her. If she'd said George was an alien I couldn't have been more surprised. Mum – living with someone when she'd always been so bloody scathing about anyone else setting up – living in sin, as she called it – before they were married.

'But we . . . it's so small here!' I said weakly, trying to imagine what it would be like having another person in the flat: George in the bathroom, George to be cooked for, George hogging the TV controls, George wanting Mum to go out places with him, George's washing, George's ironing, George's stuff all round the place. We could barely manage as it was.

'I hope we'll be able to move quite soon,' George said.

'That's right,' said Mum. 'We're looking out for a house with a garden.' When I didn't make noises of pleasure and appreciation she added, 'A nice garden for Jack to play in.'

'Oh. Right,' I said. I couldn't quite take it in. House: OK. George: not so OK. But whether I approved or not it didn't make much difference. It was official: George was here, living with us.

'We were just hanging George's things up in the wardrobe,' Mum said.

'I haven't got much with me,' said George. 'I'll have to bide my time and pop back for the rest.'

Mum looked at me, seeming a bit embarrassed. 'George had to leave in a rush yesterday evening.'

'Spent the night in the car!' George added.

My mind spun with possibilities: moonlight flits, non-payment of rent, rows with landlords. The obvious thing just didn't occur to me.

'We said we were going to move the bedside table to make room for my trouser press,' George reminded Mum.

'Let's finish that, then,' Mum said, 'and Megan will make us a nice cup of tea.'

'I like it very strong,' George said, going back into the bedroom, 'and two sugars.'

I changed Jack first, washed his face and sat him in his high chair with a biscuit. While I was making the tea, Ellie came in. 'Mum home?' she asked.

'Yes,' I said, 'and George. He's home, too.'

'What d'you mean?' she asked, and she pulled such an extraordinarily astonished face that I started laughing.

'George. He's here. Right here in the flat.'

'*George?*'

'George est arrivée,' I said, in French that was probably wrong.

'What – he's come here to meet us?' Ellie asked.

'No, he's come to live with us.'

'Don't be stupid.'

'I'm not!'

Jack threw his biscuit on the floor and I picked it up, inspected it for fluff and gave it back to him.

'Since when?'

'Since today. I came home, heard voices in Mum's bedroom and he appeared. Mum says they're engaged.' I rolled my eyes at Ellie. 'She's got a ring.'

'What's it like? What sort of stone?'

'I don't know!' I said incredulously. 'Fancy you asking a thing like that at a time like this. I didn't even look at it.'

There was a long silence and then Ellie heaved a great sigh and shook her head. 'What a turn up. We thought he was just a bloke at work.'

'He was, apparently – until their love blossomed!'

'Don't tell me he said that?'

I nodded.

'Yuk,' we both said together.

'It's a bit strange though, isn't it?' I said in a low voice. 'He arrived all unannounced – I mean, I don't think Mum knew he was moving in today. And he told me that he's going back for more stuff later. Apparently he spent last night in his car.'

'His wife chucked him out, then,' Ellie said.

'What?'

'It's obvious, isn't it? His wife found out he was seeing Mum and chucked him out.'

I gasped. 'I bet you're right.'

'We're going to be falling over each other here with five of us!' she said, pulling an anguished face. 'What's he like, anyway?'

'Fattish. Funny hair,' I said, turning my nose up. 'Not exactly gorgeous.'

'Nor is Mum,' she pointed out.

I found a banana in the fruit bowl and started mashing it up for Jack's tea. He was getting tired, now, grizzling and giving the occasional irritable shriek. The biscuit, half-chewed, had disappeared somewhere between him and the high chair tray, and he'd rubbed some soggy bits of it into his hair. I looked at my watch. I couldn't put him to bed before six – if I did he'd be up, bouncing around, by nine o'clock. I had to keep him going until seven at least to have any chance of getting him through the night.

Ellie looked out of the kitchen and towards Mum's bedroom. 'Suppose we hate him?'

I shrugged. 'Dunno. If we do . . . I suppose we'll just have to put up with him.'

It was an hour later and we were sitting down for what was normally called 'tea' but what Mum had today called 'supper'. Ellie had been sent down to the corner shop for a pizza and some salad, and there wasn't a sign of a chip anywhere. We were all being terribly polite and formal with our 'Please pass the salad cream' and 'Anyone want some more tomato?' except Jack, of course, who didn't know it was a Big Occasion and so was sitting under the table eating a biscuit and making the occasional rude noise.

'So, what are you doing at school, then?' George asked Ellie.

Ellie shot a look at me. She hated being asked things like that. 'Lessons,' she said.

'Ellie!' Mum said warningly.

'Well, you know. Just the usual.'

'Have you started your GCSEs yet?' George asked pleasantly.

Ellie shook her head.

'Because my daughter – Ria – is right in the middle of hers.'

Ellie and I made startled faces at each other. So he did have children! I wanted to ask how many he had, and why he wasn't living with them, but under Mum's steely glare I didn't dare.

Jack got tired of his biscuit, threw it across the floor and went under the table to find his duck. We heard a *quack-quack-quack* as he pushed it up and down between our legs, and then he emerged at the other end – George's end – and stood up, putting a sticky hand on George's smart office-sharp trousers to help pull himself up. George looked alarmed and brushed at his leg to dislodge Jack's hand. 'And why isn't this young man joining us for supper?' he asked.

'He's already had his,' I said. 'I can't keep him going that long – we eat too late.'

Jack, knowing he was being spoken about, gave George a beaming smile, and George just about managed to smile back. Jack then smacked his hand on to George's thigh. 'Man!' he said. Or something like it.

'That's right. Man! Another word!' I said delightedly to Mum and Ellie. 'That's about seven altogether now.'

I lifted Jack on to my lap and bounced him up and down. 'Clever, clever boy!'

Jack chuckled, then he turned and reached towards my plate, trying to grab the pizza. I cut him a tiny slice of it and he wriggled off my lap and went back under the table with it. Ellie and I both laughed, but Mum tutted.

'Megan!' she said, shaking her head. 'Bad habits . . . '

'Your mother's right,' George said, brushing sticky bits off his trousers. 'Neither of my children were allowed to eat anything unless they were sitting up at the table properly.'

Bully for them, I wanted so say.

'Manners can't begin too young,' he went on.

Ellie kicked me under the table and I kicked her back. Nightmare! It was going to be like having another Mum – only worse.

CHAPTER NINE

'And so he just moved in!' I said dramatically. 'I came home on Friday and there he was taking up half the flat!'

Claire and Josie gasped, giving me all their attention for the first time that evening. For ages they'd been comparing mobile phones, ringing each other and messing about text messaging, so much so that I'd begun to think that without a mobile phone I might as well be dead.

It was Sunday night and the three of us were in *California's* with all the beautiful people. Josie was wearing a short stretchy black top and snakeskin trousers and high heels, Claire was wearing similar trousers with what looked like a sparkly bikini top. I was just wearing my jeans and a T-shirt.

'It must be *lurve*,' Josie said. 'Your mum must have had some sort of brainstorm.'

Claire nodded. 'She must have got it bad. Fancy him moving in already!'

'It's really weird. I've never even *seen* her with a man before,' I said.

'Is he married?' Josie asked.

I shrugged. 'Dunno. He's *been* married, because he's got kids. And on Thursday night he said he slept in his car – so Ellie and I reckon he must have got chucked out from wherever he was living.'

'Whoo-ee!' Josie said. She stood up and I saw that a couple of boys had arrived at the bar just in front of us and she was going to try and get herself noticed. This was what the *whoo-ee* – all cute and perky, accompanied by both arms being stretched out – had been about. She'd had another tattoo done – a butterfly just below her collarbone on the right, and the low-cut top drew attention to it. The boys were all eyes, smirking and eyeing her up and down.

'I wonder what it'll be like,' Claire said. She was looking at the two boys, too, but she wasn't quite as obvious as Josie. 'I mean, you've never had anyone living with you and your mum before, have you? D'you think he'll be strict?'

I nodded. 'He is.'

'Aw, he'll be all right,' Josie said. 'My stepfather's brilliant! Like – he's got money, for a start. We were really broke before he came along, but now we go on

100

holiday and go out for meals all the time and everything. He got me my job at his firm, too.'

'I don't want to work with him and my mum in the estate agents, thank you,' I said.

'The two of them are babysitting tonight, though, aren't they?' Claire said. 'So that's something.'

I nodded, thinking that at least now he was living with us, Mum wouldn't be out so much. 'When he suggested it, I couldn't get out the door quick enough. He even lent me a fiver!'

Josie let out a cackle of laughter. 'He didn't volunteer to babysit just to be nice,' she said. 'He did it to get you out of the way.'

I looked at her, not knowing what she was getting at.

'You cramp their style!' she said. 'Bet your sister's out too, eh?'

I nodded.

'Well, then. They want a little bit of nookie, don't they?' She glanced over to the two boys to make sure they were watching her and added loudly, 'A touch-up in front of the telly!' before collapsing in giggles.

I thought about it. It wasn't a nice thought. Not Mum and him. In fact, it made me cringe . . .

'Bet they are!' Josie went on. 'They'll be at it

hammer and tongs by now. Don't go home early – you might get a shock!'

'Just because your mum and dad are always at it!' Claire put in. 'I don't suppose everyone else's are.'

'My mum and dad even did it on the stairs, once,' Josie said proudly.

'How d'you know?' I asked.

'My brother saw them.' She shrieked with laughter again. 'Don't look all disgusted, Megan Warrell. You've done it – why shouldn't they? I think it's nice that they still want to do it.'

I thought about this; I didn't think it was particularly nice. 'Anyway, we haven't got stairs in our flat,' I said.

We began to talk about something else. Josie was staring at the two boys openly now. She might as well have had a notice on her forehead saying, *I'm Josie and I'm up for it*. She got what she wanted, though, because after ten minutes or so of blatant staring, giggling and posturing, the boys came over, asked if we wanted drinks, and then went back to the bar to get them.

While they were getting the drinks I found out that Claire and Josie had seen them there before, but had never managed to get them over. I was instructed to call both girls by different names: Chelsea and Jonquil, to pretend that they had jobs in a PR agency – and on pain of death to keep quiet about the fact that Claire was still at school. I began to wonder where I was going to fit into this foursome.

The boys came back with drinks and sat down, and told us that their names were Pete and Lou. I thought they looked pretty OK. I mean, I wouldn't have tried to poach them or anything – not that they were going to fancy me in a grey T-shirt which smelt slightly of baby-sick – and not after all the hard work that had gone into getting them over. Anyway, even if I *had* gone for it with either of them I was put straight out of the running by Josie announcing that I might have to go home early because I had a baby to look after.

Pete and Lou turned to me in surprise. 'Yeah?'

I nodded, embarrassed to be in the spotlight. 'He's just over a year old. His name's Jack.'

'Phew!' Pete said, and immediately made a dismissive gesture with his hand, as much as to say leave him out of it.

'Aah, it's a dear ickle baby-waby,' Josie said, screwing up her face into a stupid expression.

'I got a little brother called Jack,' Lou said, but that was about the last thing they said to me. The five of us got up and had a dance or two together, but a bit after that Lou and Claire went up to the bar and started chatting to each other up there, and Pete and Josie began dancing very slowly and sexily, arms around each other.

I sat there for a while, smiling glassily at nothing in particular. Then I went to the loo for ages, then I walked around seeing if there might possibly be someone else there I knew. Suppose – just suppose – Jon had been there. How good would *that* have been? Of course he wasn't, though. I sat down again, wishing I'd brought a book with me.

I didn't feel right in there. I didn't fit in. It wasn't just I didn't have my nails done with little sparkly stones sticking on them, or a tattoo on my shoulder, or snakeskin trousers or the latest shoes, it was more than that. All *this* lot were all in some vast, special gang. They could chat up, get chatted up, have dates, flirt, two-time, sleep with whoever they wanted, if they wanted. They had nothing else in the world to worry about except themselves. Me? I couldn't do anything – anything – without having a big debate with myself first. Should I be doing this? Could I afford it? Could I fit it into my life? What about Jack? Would whatever-it-was affect him?

As I sat there I began to feel sorry for myself. I'd missed out on a big chunk of my life. Never, ever again was I going to be the same as the other girls there. I'd known this ever since Jack was born, of course, but could usually push it to the back of my mind – when I was shopping, or cooking, or cleaning it didn't matter. Here, though, I had to face up to how different I was.

The lonelier I felt, the more I missed Jack. I watched 'Chelsea' and 'Jonquil' falling all over the two boys and wondered what he was doing. He'd been fast asleep when I'd left – had he woken up again and missed me? He was OK with Mum if I wasn't around, but what with the broken nights he was having lately, neither of us was much good at getting him back to sleep.

I looked at my watch. It was only ten o'clock and I'd told Mum and George that I'd be home on the last bus, which didn't go until five past eleven. I couldn't go yet. And anyway, hadn't I been desperate to get out for ages? If I went home early wouldn't I regret it later, when I was warming jars of baby food or folding sleeping suits or sorting out the airing cupboard?

I sat with a rigid smile on my face, looking into the distance as if I could see something extremely interesting in the shadows. When any of the four looked over to me I waved cheerily or pulled a face or did something which meant I was having a bloody good time.

By ten-fifteen I couldn't stand it any longer. Even if what Josie had said was true, it would be OK to go home now because Ellie was due in at ten, so I wasn't going to interrupt anything. I said goodbye to the others – by true mistake calling Josie by her real name instead of Jonquil – and set off.

Back at the flats, Witch's Brew had just come out of her friend's flat on our floor. It was uncanny really, any coming and going anywhere in our block and she seemed to be there.

'How's the new addition to your household?' she asked.

'Jack? I've had him over a year now,' I said, deliberately misunderstanding her.

'I don't mean Jack – I mean your mum's fancy man. Settled in, has he?'

I grinned to myself. 'Yes, I think so.'

'Be getting crowded in your place now.'

'It is a bit.'

'Still, maybe he'll be buying you a new house soon.'

'That'd be nice,' I said, opening the front door.

I was just going to shout out hello when Mum called, 'Is that you, Megan? About time!'

'What d'you mean? I'm early!' I called back, and then there was a thump as Jack jumped down from the sofa and ran along the corridor towards me. He made a noise that was something like 'Moom!', hurled his arms around my legs and hugged me tight, and I felt the funny mixture of delight and exasperation that I always felt when I came in and he clung on to me. A part of me was thrilled that he was so pleased to see me, but the other part was irritated at him acting as if I'd been to the Himalayas for six weeks when I'd only been out of the house a couple of hours.

George came out into the hall. 'We've had one *hell* of an evening.'

'Why?' I asked.

'That child of yours. The door had hardly closed behind you before he was out of bed. And d'you think your mother and I could get him back to sleep again?'

I went past him into the sitting room, Jack still clinging on to me. 'Where's Ellie?'

'Gone to bed,' Mum said. 'We really have had an awful time of it. As soon as he knew you weren't around he started playing up.'

I sat down and lifted Jack on to my lap. He immediately put his head on my shoulder. 'Bye-byes,' he said.

'He's not really been naughty, then – just awake?'

'Your mother and I were hoping for a nice quiet night to ourselves,' George said humpily.

'You'll really have to ask the health visitor about his sleeping pattern,' Mum said. 'We can't have this night after night.'

'He was only bad tonight because I wasn't in,' I said defensively.

'But he nearly always wakes up in the evenings now. Several times, sometimes.'

'It's just a stage he's going through.' I stood up, hoisting Jack on to my shoulder. 'I'll put him down now,' I said. 'And then I'll go to bed myself.'

I said goodnight – I'd stopped kissing Mum goodnight over the last few days because I didn't fancy having to kiss George, too – and went into my bedroom. Ellie was in bed, listening to music on her headphones. I pointed outside and made a face and she took the headphones off. 'He wasn't that bad,' she said. 'Just running about a bit.'

'What time did you get in?'

'Just after ten.' She screwed up her nose. 'It was

weird. As I was coming into the flats it seemed . . . funny. As if it wasn't our flat any more.'

I put Jack into his cot, laid his blanket next to him and tucked his duvet round him. 'I know what you mean,' I said. 'It's because of George, isn't it?' I bent to kiss Jack, saying, 'Night-night, Jack, see you in the morning' in the right, firm way, then sat on the bed to take off my make-up (which was actually Ellie's make-up). 'Maybe it won't last very long,' I whispered. 'Mum and George, I mean.'

'Bet it does,' Ellie said gloomily. 'She's never had a boyfriend before so she's going to hang on to him.'

I shrugged. 'So if she wants him around, what can we do?'

'Nothing,' Ellie said.

Outside in the hall I could hear low talk and foot-steps as Mum and George got ready for bed. 'I'm glad our bedroom's not right next to theirs,' I said to Ellie.

'Why?'

'*You* know,' I said. 'Noises.'

'Noises?' She sat up on one elbow and looked at me, puzzled, and I thought, God, she doesn't know what I mean. She might go in for a spot of snogging but she's still only twelve. 'Oh, nothing,' I said.

I hung a scarf over our bedside light to kill it a little

and help Jack go to sleep.

'Did you go to that *California* place then? Did you have a good time?'

'Yeah. Great,' I said automatically, and then I thought about it and added, 'No. Not really. It was a bit of a dead loss.'

There was a scuffling noise from Jack's cot and a rattle of the cot bars as he pulled himself up. I groaned to myself. I'd been thinking about putting up some sort of curtain affair so that when Jack was in his cot he couldn't see me, but I hadn't yet worked out how to do it.

'Momomomo,' he said, waving at me.

'Ssshh! Bedtime!' I said. I turned off the light, laid down and closed my eyes, and after a while Jack did the same. I then lay there like a dead lump, scared to go and clean my teeth or even *move* in case it disturbed him. In the end he fell asleep and I did, too.

CHAPTER TEN

'Whatever's that child got on?' Mum said as I carried Jack into the kitchen for breakfast.

'Give it a rest, Mum,' I said.

'Well – what *is* it?'

'It's called a bandana.' I sat Jack in his high chair and adjusted the red cotton scarf over Jack's forehead. 'And doesn't he look gorgeous in it?'

'He looks ridiculous!'

'Perhaps he's supposed to be a pirate,' George said with a smirk, sitting down at the kitchen table. 'All he needs is an earring.'

Mum turned to look at me. 'I hope you wouldn't ever think of having his ears pierced, Megan.'

'Don't worry, I can't afford it,' I said, adding milk to Jack's breakfast cereal and stirring it. I'd been thinking about an earring since Josie had once suggested it, but couldn't decide whether they were super cool or just plain common. 'Anyway, I'd only have one ear done,' I added.

'Ghastly,' Mum shuddered. She put a plate of toast in front of George, and he was just stretching across the table for the butter when Jack suddenly kicked up his legs, striking the underneath of his high chair tray. The tray, holding a full bowl of porridge, went up in the air and the porridge went all over him. It also went right along the arm of George's pale blue shirt.

There was a moment's shocked silence and then George jumped up shouting, 'Oh bugger the little bastard!'

Jack, at the shock of being covered in porridge and at the harsh sound of George's voice, burst into tears.

'Don't call him that!' I said, gathering Jack up and getting covered in porridgey bits. 'It was just an accident.'

'Look at what he's done!' He got up, brushing at his sleeve. 'I'll have to go and change. Last night and now this – what a bloody fiasco!'

I rocked Jack on my lap, soothing him and shooting a look of hatred at George. 'He didn't do it deliberately – he was just kicking his legs around. And there's no need for you to shout at him.'

'Well, he is, isn't he? He is exactly what I called him,' George said, and he went out, slamming the door behind him.

'Mum!' I protested
I'm not having him ta

Mum carried on w
lost his temper, that's
men are like. He didn'

'Oh, but he did. He

'He was just cross,
did have an awful time

'It was you who offe

By the time I'd changed us both, given Jack his breakfast and collected the one hundred and one things I needed for the day, my taxi had been waiting ten minutes. Consequently I had to hear a tirade about 'I ought to get waiting time, the amount of time I waste hanging around' and 'You'd think if people were getting free taxis everywhere at least they'd know not to keep them waiting'.

I didn't say anything. I could have started a row but just couldn't be bothered, so I sat there and stared out of the window. I should have been saying 'car', 'tree', 'dog', 'woman' and so on, but I was too utterly fed up. Why was my life so boring, so samey? Why were there such *losers* in it? Why didn't someone like Heathcliff (I'd decided that yes, he was untamed and passionate) come along on a black horse, throw me gallop off over the moors?

got to Poppies I went to find Kirsty,
the nursery with Stella, giving her a

easier to feed her here than in my grotty
m,' she said. 'And at least I can warm the bottle
up.'

'Did you have any luck with finding somewhere to stay?'

She shook her head. 'I spoke to my landlady and she said they can't put the redecorating off for any longer.' She heaved a sigh. 'They're only saying that to get me out, though. I know they are. I bet they don't do any work on my room at all.'

She finished feeding Stella, then sat her up and winded her. 'Does she look OK?' she asked me anxiously. 'I've put her best things on her. I don't want Vicki to think I'm not looking after her properly.'

'She looks fine to me,' I said, although actually the little stretch suit the baby was wearing didn't look all that clean. I knew Kirsty didn't have a washing machine, she'd told me before that she just hand-washed in the basin in her room. 'Do you need any baby clothes?' I asked her. 'Only I've got loads of old stuff of Jack's – sleeping suits and so on. He only wore his newborn clothes a few times because he grew so quickly. Do you want me to look some things out for you?'

Kirsty nodded. 'Brilliant. Thanks.'

'I won't be needing them myself for a long, long time,' I said, thinking that the next time I got pregnant I was going to have all new things. My stuff was OK, but most of it had been second- or third-hand from charity shops or jumble sales. Next time it was going to be different, planned. The next baby would have the best of everything.

'Where d'you think you're going to live, then?' I asked. I settled Jack down with Sinna's baby, and they began to pull at a threadbare teddy.

Kirsty shook her head. 'I don't know,' she said. 'I was thinking that my landlady couldn't possibly throw me out on the street, so if I just tell her that I've got nowhere to go then I might be allowed to stay there.'

'But what about them trying to keep you out of the kitchen?' I said, 'and what about them complaining about Stella crying all the time?'

'Well, she won't cry so much as she gets older, will she?'

'Don't you believe it,' I said.

She shook her head. 'I don't know. I just don't

know what to do . . . ' All the time she was speaking she was patting Stella on the back. Suddenly the baby coughed and brought up what looked like half her feed all down her. Some of it went on to her bib, but most of it went all over the stretch suit. Startled, Stella coughed again and started crying.

Kirsty looked at me in anguish. 'Oh no! She'll be hungry again now – and I've only got one more bottle for the day. And I didn't bring her a change of clothes, either!'

I was about to start rummaging for something of Jack's to lend her when Marie, one of the nursery nurses, came over. 'Never mind,' she said. 'I'll take Stella off and give her a little bath, shall I?'

As Stella was whisked away, Kirsty's bottom lip trembled. 'I can't do anything right, can I? I can't even feed my own baby without her being sick.'

'Don't be daft,' I said. 'Jack's been sick millions of times. It's what they like doing best – being sick!'

She tried to smile. 'What shall I do about another bottle, though?'

'They'll be able to mix you up one here. And they've got loads of baby clothes to put her in. It'll be OK!'

She smiled again, but her eyes were full of tears

and they brimmed over. 'Sorry,' she said. 'I know I keep crying all the time but I'm just really tired. I was awake all last night trying to stop Stella screaming. I really wanted everything to be all right today, too. I wanted Vicki to see that I could cope.' She gave a sob. 'And now everything's going wrong and they'll tell Vicki that Stella was sick and everything!'

'That's nothing!' I said. 'Really. We all have bad days.'

'All my days are bad days,' Kirsty said.

She went off to help bath Stella and I went off to an English lesson. Later in the morning I was in one of the study rooms waiting for my tutor when Vicki came in.

'I know Kirsty is a particular friend of yours so I wanted you to know that she won't be coming here for a little while,' she said.

I looked at Vicki in surprise. 'Why not?'

'We're giving her a break. We think trying to cope on her own is all a bit much for her, so she's going to live with a foster mother for a while.'

'And Stella as well?' I asked immediately.

'In a week or so, yes,' Vicki said. She hesitated. 'We hope – I very much hope – that they'll be living together again soon.'

'But why . . . what's happening now, then?'

'Well, it's felt by Social Services that Stella is in need of a little more care. She's going to be taken into the baby unit of a hospital for a few days to be fed up and to get into some sort of routine. And then she and Kirsty will live with a foster mother who'll be able to give Kirsty some mothering experience and get them off on the right foot. Kirsty's just not ready to be completely on her own with Stella at the moment.'

'Where is she now, then?' I asked, because I hadn't seen any comings and goings. 'Has she gone already?'

Vicki nodded. 'They've gone off to the hospital.'

'I didn't know,' I said, meaning that she hadn't come and said goodbye to me.

'Kirsty was quite upset,' Vicki said, 'so we didn't want her disturbing everyone else. She's going to settle Stella at the hospital and collect her stuff from her lodgings before she goes to her new place. Then she can get sorted out before Stella joins her.'

I bit my lip. It could happen, then: they could take babies away. The thought was so scary that I felt like snatching up Jack there and then and rushing off with him.

'It's OK,' Vicki said gently, 'I know what you're thinking but she will get Stella back. Social Services don't intend to steal her away and keep her.'

'Kirsty will be so miserable without her,' I said.

'I know,' Vicki said, 'but although Kirsty's a lovely girl, she's very young and she does need a little extra help. It's for her sake as much as anyone's – we don't want her to end up with post-natal depression. The ideal thing would be for her to live with her own mum, but as that's not possible, everyone thinks this is the best solution.'

'Can't Kirsty's own mum be *made* to have her back?' I burst out, but Vicki was shaking her head before I'd even finished the sentence.

'That would be no good, would it? Kirsty's life would be even more miserable living with someone who didn't want her.'

'So when she's settled with the foster mother, will she be able to come back here during the day?'

Vicki nodded. 'I hope so. She'll be living out of the area but I think we can get something sorted out. In the meantime I'll try and find out the phone number of where she'll be living so you can keep in touch.'

The other girls and I talked about Kirsty at lunch break and everyone said that if they were in any diffi-culties they would never tell anyone.

'Bet she doesn't get that baby back,' Stacey said darkly.

'Bet it's just taken away and adopted,' Hannah added.

I shook my head. 'I don't think so. I don't think Vicki would let it happen.'

'It's nothing to do with Vicki,' Stacey said. 'She's just in charge *here*. It's all down to social workers, see. They're always watching. You blow your nose the wrong way and they'll be on to you.'

We all laughed. 'They've been OK with me, though,' I said. 'In fact, I haven't seen any social workers since I was pregnant.'

'That's because you're living at home with your mum,' Hannah said. 'If you weren't, they'd be watching your every move.'

Stacey looked down at her engagement ring proudly. 'As soon as I started living with Eliot they were on to me,' she said, 'checking him out and making sure he was OK. Nearly frightened him off, they did. You wait till you start living with someone,' she said to me.

'Chance would be a fine thing,' I said, pulling a face. 'I haven't had a boyfriend since I got pregnant.'

Two or three of the others shook their heads and said they hadn't either.

'Mind you, there's a boy who goes to that school round here who's chatted to me a few times . . . ' I said.

Two of the girls went off to play at painting with their toddlers but Michelle hung back. 'A couple of boys from that school were hanging around last year,' she said. 'One was called Jason and one was Jon.'

I looked at her. 'Spelt J-O-N?'

She nodded and grinned. 'Fit bloke. But you know why he hangs around here, don't you?'

I shook my head, though I thought I knew already what she was going to say.

'Because we're sex on a plate, of course. We've put it out once so we're bound to do it again. And all without too much effort on his part.'

I had to laugh. 'He wishes!' I hesitated. 'Did you go out with him?'

'No,' she said. 'But not being funny – I could have done. He made it clear that he wasn't interested in a proper relationship, though. Just the business.'

That was it, then. My one chance of romance gone. 'Yeah, I thought it might be like that,' I said. But I'd been hoping it wouldn't be.

I was in a right mood that afternoon. If Jon had showed up I would have cut him dead – and if the taxi driver had started I would have had a right go at him.

Jon didn't appear, though, and Mr Creep was morose and silent all the way home.

That left George – the other man in my life. If he started on me or Jack again that evening, I decided I was going to let rip. How dare he upset us? If he wanted to live with us he ought to be on his best behaviour – at least at the beginning. If he lost his temper again I was going to have to have a serious talk to Mum and say we shouldn't have to put up with it.

But then, I thought, what if they said that I should be the one to go? What if Mum told me I had to get a single-mum bedsitter or something because she wanted to be with George? It did happen. I knew that now.

All this was going through my head as I let myself into the flat. Unusually, they were both home before me, sitting together on the sofa all cosy. I said hello, looked at them both coldly and went into the kitchen to make Jack's tea.

George came in after me.

'Sorry about this morning,' he said. 'I was feeling a bit stressed out. I'm going through a funny old time at the moment.'

'That's OK,' I muttered, not meaning it.

'Your mum and I have got something exciting to

tell you,' he went on, and then Mum came through waving some sheets of paper.

'Guess what?'

I shrugged, pretending disinterest. They weren't going to win me over that easily.

She took Jack from me and gave me the papers. 'Look at these, Megan. See what you think.'

I looked. It was estate agent's details of a house on the other side of town. 'What's this for?'

'Well, we've been to look at that house today,' George began.

'It's lovely and we're having it!' Mum said.

'What?!'

'George and I are buying a house together! You read the details, Megan. It's got four bedrooms – that's one each for you and Ellie and a bedroom of his own for Jack.' She swung Jack round in her arms. 'Your own bedroom, Jack! And a garden with a swing in it. What d'you think about that?'

I looked. It seemed OK – better than OK. And I thought maybe I wouldn't say anything to rock the boat.

'Hey! You avoiding me or something?' Jon said as I stepped out of Poppies on Wednesday.

For a tiny moment I went all fluttery – and then, as I remembered what Michelle had said, the flutteriness disappeared. I put my face into polite-but-disinterested. 'No,' I shrugged.

He grinned at me. His hair was growing now, so his head was softly furry all over, like velvet. 'Only I came up here early two days ago, specially early to see you, but I reckon you saw me coming and went indoors again.'

I shrugged. 'I don't remember.' I shifted Jack from one arm to the other – I couldn't put him down on the grass because it had been raining and everything was soaking wet.

Jack waved a chubby arm towards Jon. 'Man!' he said, giving one of his big, beautiful smiles.

'That's right,' I said. 'Man.'

Jon grinned at him. 'He's dead cute, isn't he?'

'Absolutely the cutest,' I said. I looked down the road for my taxi. Why did it never come when I wanted it?

'So, Gorgeous, are we going to have this date, then?'

The slight flutteriness came back again and I quickly squashed it. 'I didn't know we were having one.'

'We chatted about it a week or so back. You told me where you lived and I said I'd find out about trains.'

'Did you?'

He looked at me, head on one side, brown eyes narrowed. 'Are you going chilly on me?'

I gave him a vague, bewildered look. 'I didn't know I was hot. I don't really know you, do I?' And then added, before I could stop myself, 'Although Michelle speaks very highly of you.'

'Ah,' he said, grinning. 'That's it, is it? You've been chatting about me. Come out of it well, did I?'

I could have kicked myself. *Now* he'd think that he was the number one topic of conversation. To save myself from having to reply, I got a tissue out of my pocket and started to wipe fussily around Jack's mouth. Jack spluttered and squawked and wriggled, while I pretended to be intent on my task.

Jon went on, 'Anyway, what I wanted to say was – I'm taking my driving test at the weekend and if I pass my mum says she'll lend me her car. I could drive over and see you if you like. Take you out somewhere.'

Michelle's words drifted off into the ether and the flutteriness came back full on. *A date*! Going out with someone again! So what if he tried it on? I was old enough to look after myself. Old enough to say no. In my head I saw myself in a car with Jon, sitting beside him and going somewhere nice – to a restaurant, a film, a club, a party. Or McDonalds, come to that. Anywhere.

'OK,' I heard myself saying.

'Tell me where you live, give me your phone number and if I don't see you round here before the weekend, I'll ring you.'

I told him. I tried to be cool but it was hard, because I hadn't been out with anyone in *years* and it was the most exciting thing that had happened for ages. Jon, still smiling in a sort of ironic I-know-you've-been-talking-about-me way, wrote down my details on a piece of paper, gave me a wink, stroked Jack's head and went off.

'Good luck with the test!' I shouted after him, and he raised one arm in the air in a victory salute.

I watched him as he disappeared. A date at last. Not a boyfriend, necessarily – it was too early for all that stuff – but a *date*.

CHAPTER ELEVEN

I leaned back in the car, feeling soft leather against my head. This was the life: being driven around in a decent car.

'So maybe it won't be too bad having him around,' Ellie whispered to me.

'Maybe,' I said.

'At least we can go out places now.'

It was Sunday and Ellie and I were in the back of George's car, with Jack, fast asleep, in a makeshift harness on the seat between us. We were on our way home from what George had called 'a proper family day out' – which had turned out to be an afternoon really, as it had taken me so long to get Jack sorted out and ready for such an outing. We'd been heading for the seaside originally, but the weather had turned so we'd just gone into the country and had a picnic.

It was the first time I could ever remember us going on such a thing. I mean, we'd been to the local park with a couple of sausage rolls before, but this was a few notches up from that. Mum had pulled out all the stops: as well as a proper tablecloth, bottle of wine and a bowl of fruit, there were Cornish pasties and each of us had individual salads in plastic containers. I was impressed by this, but it turned out that she'd only done individual ones because George liked his salads to consist of watercress and beetroot *only* – he hated tomatoes and cucumber. 'Men!' she'd said, handing his over and pretending she was exasperated.

I closed my eyes as the car purred along. I liked having a car; we'd never had one before. Mum had always said it wasn't necessary to have a car if you lived in town, you ought to walk and save the ozone layer, but she'd stopped going on about that now that he'd had his insurance changed so that she could drive the BMW. She went everywhere in the car, even down to the corner shop.

I had, of course, been waiting for Jon to ring me all weekend. All . . . every single minute . . . of the weekend. He hadn't said what would happen if he didn't pass his test – was he going to contact me anyway? – but I thought that at least he would have phoned and let me know either way. He hadn't, though, so I was going to cut him dead when I saw him again. Absolutely cut-him-to-slices dead.

'Do you think Jack enjoyed the picnic?' Ellie asked.

I yawned, looking down at Jack, grubby, with grass stains on his knees and quite a lot of Cornish pasty round his face. 'I think so. It's difficult to tell. I mean, babies aren't that good at sitting down on a rug and admiring the view, are they?'

Ellie giggled. 'Or sitting down at all, really.'

All Jack had wanted to do was walk across the tablecloth (he didn't seem to be able to tell where blanket stopped and table began), fall on to people's food or make grabs at their drinks. When he wasn't doing this he was falling into bushes or cowpats or making wild breaks for freedom, thinking it was huge fun to gallop off into the distance and head towards the river.

'I'm sure he liked it,' I said to Ellie. 'And it's good for him to see different places. I don't want him to grow up to be one of those kids who's never seen a cow.'

'He didn't see one today,' she said.

'You know what I mean.'

George clicked the indicator of his car and it pulled off the road, crunching over a gravel drive into the car park of a hotel. It was an old place, covered with ivy, with big trees surrounding it and a conservatory crammed with hanging vines. 'Ooh,' Mum said, staring around. 'This looks nice. Why have we come in here?'

'I thought we might have a drink,' George said. 'One for the road.'

Ellie and I exchanged raised-eyebrow glances. This was a new thing for us: a swish hotel, drinks in the conservatory, gracious living. I looked down at what I was wearing: jeans. Was I posh enough? Was Ellie? My glance fell on Jack.

'What about Jack?' I asked anxiously. 'He's fast asleep.'

George's eyes looked into mine in the driver's mirror. 'I was thinking about a drink for me and your mum,' he said. 'Just the two of us.'

'Can't we come in as well?' Ellie pleaded.

The car came to rest under a tree and George's hand went down over Mum's. 'Just a quiet treat for the adults,' he said to her, and then added in quite a different tone, 'After the day we've had with you lot I think we deserve it.'

I looked at Ellie, open-mouthed and she looked back at me, equally stunned. Gracious living – but not for us.

Mum looked over her shoulder at me and said,

rather quickly, 'We won't be long, girls. Just a swift one, eh, George?'

'Just a swift one or three,' George said wittily. He got out and rolled down his window, peering in at us. 'Never let it be said that I leave children or animals in a car with the windows up!'

They went off and I turned to Ellie. 'The cheek!'

'Fancy leaving us in here!'

Jack opened his eyes and began to whimper. 'Oh, brilliant,' I said. 'He's woken up in a mood.'

'I bet he'll want changing,' Ellie said, sniffing the air. 'Where are his things?'

'All in the boot.' I tried the doors – they opened. 'At least he hasn't left us here with the child locks on,' I said.

We undid our seat belts and released Jack. 'He's treating us like servants,' I said, looking out resentfully at the glories of the hotel. 'He doesn't think we're good enough to go inside.'

'Big lump!' Ellie said. She hesitated. 'Megan,' she asked thoughtfully. 'D'you think George likes us?'

'Dunno,' I said as I battled with Jack, who, hot and fretful, was struggling to get down on the floor.

'I get the idea that he doesn't.'

'He probably resents us being around,' I said. 'He'd

like to have Mum all to himself.'

'Oh, *would* he,' Ellie said. 'Well, he's not going to.'

I thought, stupidly, that when we got home there might be a message from Jon. OK, I was absolutely going to cut him dead, but a note pushed through the door, or a small bunch of flowers left on the doorstep, would have been nice. We didn't have an answer-phone so there was no possibility of a message being left, and one half of me thought what does it matter – sod him – and the other half said consolingly that he'd been trying to ring all afternoon but we'd been out.

When the phone rang about fifteen minutes after we'd got home I was bathing Jack and couldn't get to it. I listened at the bathroom door, positive it was for me. Ellie shouted it was for George, though, and then I heard him come into the hall and close the sitting room door firmly behind him.

'Oh, it's you, is it? How did you find this number?' I heard him say, and then there was a series of grunts and swear words and he said, 'Couldn't care less. You try it and see what happens!' and slammed the phone down.

I took my ear away from the door and went back to the bath, where Jack was bashing at his yellow duck, trying to drown it. Who had that been on the phone? George's ex-wife? Or was she still his wife? One of his children?

The phone rang again before George had even had time to reach the sitting-room door. He snatched it up and said, 'Look – piss off, right!' and then, 'Oh. I see. Sorry, I thought it was someone else.'

The receiver went down on the table and he called, 'Megan!'

I opened the bathroom door. 'Who is it?' I asked. It was Jon, obviously, and I was going to play it cool.

'Someone called Kirsty,' George said. He was breathing heavily and looked angry.

'Oh. Right.' I shouted for Ellie, asking her to please keep an eye on Jack in the bath, and went to take the call, feeling disappointed and pleased at the same time.

'Was it all right to ring?' Kirsty asked.

''Course!'

'Only – that man – is he your stepfather?'

'No,' I said. 'Just Mum's boyfriend.'

'He sounded really angry.'

'Oh, don't worry about him,' I said. 'How are you? What have you been doing?'

'I've left the B and B and moved to this woman's

house now. Mrs Wilson. She's a foster mother,' Kirsty said.

'Bet it was great to get out of that place, wasn't it?'

'Mmm,' Kirsty said uncertainly.

'What's this Mrs Wilson like, then?'

'All right,' Kirsty said in a low voice. 'But she's not very friendly. She keeps talking about how much it costs to keep me there. She doesn't like me to eat too much. All I had last night was a plate of chips.'

'What about Stella?'

'She's still in hospital. She's not having any treatment or anything, though. She's just being built up a bit.' Kirsty's voice lifted. 'I go every day to see her. She's looking so lovely. She's putting on weight all the time.'

'And she'll come and live with you at this foster mother's place, will she?'

'That's the idea,' Kirsty said. 'And it shouldn't be too long before we get a place of our own.'

'That'll be good,' I said, though I wasn't sure if it would be. A girl I knew – Izzy, who'd had two babies – lived in a local authority flat which was the horriblest, grottiest place I'd ever been to. Although, thinking back, that might have been more Izzy and not so much the flat.

'I've just got to prove to them that I can look after her on my own,' Kirsty went on earnestly. 'I've got to do everything right. If I don't, I've just got an awful feeling that they'll keep her. Get her adopted by someone. A proper couple.'

''Course they won't! They wouldn't be able to do that!'

Kirsty's voice shook. 'I think they can. They can do anything they want.'

'Well . . . ' I tried to think of something to say that would cheer her up, and failed. 'Chin up,' I said weakly.

I put the phone down and, very thoughtful, went back into the bathroom. Ellie had got Jack out of the bath and he was sitting on her lap, pink and glowing and gorgeous.

'He said, "Duck"!' Ellie reported. 'He pointed at it in the bath and said, "Duck".'

I smiled. 'He's a little genius!' I said, taking him from her and sitting on the side of the bath with him. I lowered my voice. 'Here,' I said, 'who was that on the phone for George?'

'A woman,' Ellie said.

'I heard him having a right go at her! He was swearing and all sorts – and then when Kirsty rang he told her to piss off.'

'Bet it was his wife who rang!' Ellie said.

As she spoke the phone began ringing again. It rang and rang but neither George nor Mum answered it.

'You go!' I said to Ellie. 'Find out if it's her.'

Ellie went into the hall. 'Who is it, please?' I heard her ask politely. She came back past the bathroom, grinning all over her face. 'It *is* her,' she whispered. 'She said, "It's Mrs Simpson."'

Ellie carried on down the hall, opened the sitting-room door and said, 'I've got someone on the phone for you, George.'

'I'm not in,' George said abruptly, and I heard Mum murmur something in the background before Ellie closed the door again.

'I'll take it,' I said to Ellie. I passed Jack to her and picked up the receiver. 'I'm afraid he's not in.'

'Well, I know he is,' the woman said. 'And you can just tell him from me that unless I get some money, I'm going to take him to court and ruin him. The bastard!' She slammed the receiver down.

'I heard that!' Ellie said in a gleeful whisper.

'So it's *him* who's the bastard,' I said. 'Who's going to tell him?'

'Not me,' Ellie said, and we both dissolved into giggles.

CHAPTER TWELVE

'We've changed our phone number,' I said to Lorna early on Wednesday morning. 'So I'm just ringing to give you the new one.'

'Why have you done that?'

'Well . . . ' I took a breath and went on to explain about George moving in, and then about the phone calls from his wife – there had been about five the day before – and about Mum contacting the telephone people, changing our number and going ex-directory.

'Your mum has moved a man in! There's hope for me yet,' Lorna said. She laughed. 'I don't mean that like it sounded – I meant that I just can't imagine your mum with a boyfriend.'

'He's hardly Brad Pitt,' I said. 'He's fat and bald.'

'What's he like as a person, though? Nice?'

I pulled a face, even though she couldn't see me. 'Not really. Ellie and I don't much like him.'

'Oh dear,' Lorna said. 'Your mum does, though, and I suppose that's what counts.'

'Yeah,' I said uncertainly.

'Is she happier?'

'She's . . . different. They go out places – he takes her shopping and to work and everything. And she can drive his car and we go out for picnics. He does things round the house, too – sorts out dripping taps and fixes curtain rails and all that. Men's things.'

'But?'

'But he makes Ellie and I feel we're in the way. And I don't think he likes babies, either.'

'Aah!' Lorna said, her voice warming. 'How is my darling?'

'He's fine,' I said. 'A new word every week now. The latest is duck.'

'Clever lad!'

'But something else – Mum's put the flat on the market and she and George are buying a house together!'

'No!'

'It's got a garden and four bedrooms and Jack's going to have his own room – we're all going to have our own rooms,' I said. 'There's loads of space!'

'It'll be *lovely* for you,' Lorna said.

'Apart from George being there.'

'Well, you won't be around that much longer, will

you?' Lorna went on. 'Another couple of years and you'll fly the nest and take Jack with you, and then Ellie will go and your mum would be on her own. At least now you won't have to worry about her being lonely without you all.'

'I s'pose not,' I said.

'Um . . . ' She hesitated. 'Have you seen Mark at all?'

'He popped in a couple of weeks ago, on a Sunday night,' I said. 'But we haven't seen him since.'

'I've written to him to ask him up here.' She sighed. 'He hasn't replied, though.'

'He said he was really busy on the newspaper,' I lied.

'I know he finds it difficult – finds coping with me difficult, I mean. Have you had a chance to say anything to him?'

'Not really,' I said. 'Not lately.'

'I know you will when you can,' she said wistfully. 'Do a good PR job on me, won't you?'

''Course I will. I always do!'

'I've joined this group of women now who've had their babies adopted. We talk about how we feel and try and iron out our guilt.' She sighed again. 'Someone said last week that it won't be until Mark has children of his own that he realises just how I feel about him.'

I didn't know what to say. Every time I spoke to her she turned the subject round to Mark, wanting to know what he was doing, longing for me to say he'd mentioned her – just wanting some sort of recognition from him. I knew, though, that Mark felt that she hadn't tried hard enough to keep him; felt that she should have held on to him no matter what. I'd told him lots of times that it was different in those days – that young mums didn't get the support that we did now, and she'd had really hard pressure put on her to have him adopted, but it didn't seem to make any difference. In Mark's eyes she'd rejected him, and that was that.

'I'd better go now,' I said to Lorna. 'We've got someone coming round to look at the flat tonight and I promised Mum that I'd clear up before I left. And you know what she's like.'

'That hasn't changed, then,' Lorna said. 'And are you getting on all right at your educational place? How's the studying coming along?'

'Fine,' I said.

'Any sort of romance in your life?'

'None at all,' I said. I still hadn't seen or heard

from Jon and I didn't want to. Didn't even want to think about him.

'Join the club,' Lorna said. 'Have a good day and give my love to Mark when you see him, won't you?'

''Course I will!'

'And to George!' she called just before I put the phone down.

As if.

'Late again,' Mr Creep said as I got in.

'Only two minutes.'

'Eight. This is a no-waiting zone. If I get caught and charged, who's going to pay the fine?'

'I don't know,' I said, thinking that if he could be bothered to get off his backside and come along the passage to give me a hand with Jack and all my stuff, as my last driver had done, then it would speed things up.

'That's just the trouble,' he said. 'No one knows. No one cares. You single girls with your fancy ideas and kids that the state has to pay for – *you* don't care, do you?'

I looked out of the window. Why don't you just shut it, I thought. I took Jack's hand and pointed as a mounted policeman went by. 'Horse,' I said.

'Duck!' said Jack. Which cheered me up a bit.

I did a survey on stepfathers that lunchtime at Poppies. Out of the seven girls there, five had them. Of those five, only one liked hers. The rest had just learned to live with them. Stacey said hers never stayed long enough to be stepfathers, they were just 'Mum's friends' and came and went so quickly she hardly bothered to learn their names. 'OK, I'm exaggerating,' she said, 'but my mum is an argumentative cow and after a few months they've had enough of her and move on.'

'You've got to weigh things up,' Stacey said. 'Either your mum's on your back all the time and there's no money for anything but you've got your place to yourself – or she's occupied with a man so there's more cash around, but there's someone forever putting his oar in and interfering.'

'It's just that everything's different now,' I said. 'We've never had anyone living with us before. It never occurred to me that she would . . . I thought my mum was past it.'

Everyone laughed. 'They're never past it,' Michelle said. 'Strikes me you've been lucky to get away with it for so long.'

I shook my head. 'I just can't believe how some mums – like Kirsty's, I mean – put their boyfriends first. Before us.'

'Tell me about it,' Jo said dourly.

'What's the latest on Kirsty, then?' someone asked.

I shook my head. 'Not good. She rang me last night in tears, because Stella's got to spend extra time at the hospital while they test her for something. She's still not quite right, apparently, so they want to do some investigations.'

'See!' Stacey said. 'Once they get the babies, they hang on to 'em.'

'Yeah, but at least if they find out she's not gaining weight because of a virus or something, then they know it's not Kirsty's fault for not looking after her properly.'

Everyone nodded.

'She said she doesn't like her foster mother,' I went on. 'She only lets her watch TV up to nine o'clock and then she has to go to bed.'

'I stayed with foster parents like that before I got my flat,' Joy said. 'They treated me like I was a naughty girl. Like – you've had a baby and now you're going to be punished for it.'

A couple of our tutors came in for us then

and everyone went off to do various tasks, leaving me and Michelle in the nursery.

'Have you seen anything else of that Jon?' she asked. 'Did you give him the cold shoulder?'

'I tried to,' I said, 'but he gave it to me first. Last weekend he said he'd come over in his mum's car, but then he didn't turn up.'

'Typical,' she said.

'I mean – OK, he might not have been able to get the car or something, but he might have phoned,' I said. 'If I see him again I'm just going to blank him out.'

'You do that, girl,' Michelle said.

That very afternoon, of course, he was outside waiting. I saw him from the door and tried to duck back in again, but he'd already seen me.

'There you are!' he said. He was wearing a pale blue T-shirt and khaki shorts, though it wasn't really the weather for them. I suppose he liked the look of his legs in them – tanned and muscular, I couldn't help noticing.

'Yes, here I am,' I said coolly, looking down the road for Mr Creep.

'I failed my test, didn't I.' Jon said. 'So I couldn't come over. Sorry.'

'That's OK,' I said casually. 'I was out anyway.'

'What – all the time?'

'Practically all weekend,' I said, inferring a non-stop programme of fun and jollity.

'I thought you didn't have a boyfriend?'

'It's none of your business whether I have or not,' I said. 'Besides, you haven't got to have a fella in your life to enjoy yourself.'

'So you haven't, then?'

I didn't reply.

'I find it hard to believe you're on your own.' He looked over Jack's head and into my eyes. 'Someone like you. You're far and away the prettiest girl here.'

'Yeah, yeah,' I said.

'Look, I really am sorry I couldn't come over, right? I had an awful weekend – failed my test, then had too much to drink and got slaughtered for it by my dad. I just didn't feel like seeing anyone.' He tried to take my hand but I pulled it away. 'Not even some-one like you.'

'Don't worry about it,' I said stiffly. Much to my horror I knew I was warming towards him, forgiving him. I could feel it happening and didn't want it to.

'You're still miffed, aren't you?'

'No. Why should I be?'

'You waited in all weekend for me to come over, didn't you?'

'No, I didn't!' I said indignantly. Talk about being sure of himself!

He took Jack's hand and swung it. 'Tell your mum I really like her,' he said to Jack.

Jack chuckled.

'She doesn't believe me,' he went on to Jack. 'She thinks I'm spinning her a line, but I'm not.'

'You won't get round me like that!' I said sharply, and then, to my relief, my taxi squealed around the corner and drew up.

Jon opened the cab door for me and, with as much dignity as I could, I clambered in with bags, changing mat, Jack and all. As I sat down, I could see Mr Creep staring at me in the mirror.

'See you sometime,' I said to Jon, very coolly.

'See you *soon*,' Jon said.

We drove off.

'We haven't seen him lately, have we?' the taxi driver said. 'So it's all on again, is it? Was it a lover's tiff?'

I pretended to be busy with Jack.

'What was it about, then?' he persisted. 'Anything I can help you with?'

'No thanks,' I muttered.

'Man of the world, me. Not much I couldn't tell you about. What was it – something he wanted to do and something you didn't?'

I felt myself going hot. I told myself that he didn't mean *that*.

'Lot of trouble caused by those sorts of things. Men have got their urges, see, and often women don't fulfil them.'

Just stop now, I thought.

'Straight sex is all right, but . . . '

I found my voice. 'I don't want to talk about it,' I interrupted him. 'I'm not listening.'

'Oh, get you,' he scoffed. 'No better than you should be and giving yourself airs and graces.'

'If you say anything else I'm going to report you,' I said, my voice shaking.

'Do that! See what good it does. You're nothing but a little tart – who's going to believe you?'

I picked up Jack and buried my face in his shoulder, holding on to softness, baby skin, the smell of talc and biscuits. I was so angry, so very angry. I felt I wanted to cry but I didn't want to do it in front of *him*. Sometimes I hated all men.

CHAPTER THIRTEEN

I had a bad time with Jack that night. He woke up three times and played up so much that in the end even Ellie got fed up with him. 'Can't you *do* something?' she hissed at me, and then went off in a huff to sleep on the sitting-room sofa. At one point – I think it was about two in the morning – George crashed into the bedroom and stood at the end of my bed.

He glowered at Jack, who was standing up in the cot, shaking the bars and crying. 'Is that child *ever* going to sleep?' he asked furiously.

'I don't know,' I said. 'He's teething or something.'

'For Christ's sake! Some of us have got to work in the morning!'

'It's not my fault,' I said. 'And he can't help it. Didn't your kids ever cry?'

George made a face – a sort of snarling face – at me, and then Mum called, 'George! Come back here. You won't do any good like that.' And he just glowered and went out again.

The next morning I was so tired that I couldn't get up. Jack was absolutely fast asleep by then too, so I got Mum to ring the taxi company to say I wouldn't be going in that day. I wondered if that might give him – Mr Creep – something to worry about, although I doubted it. Even if I did complain about what he'd said who would believe me? He'd just deny it and say that I'd taken it the wrong way, that he'd just been try-ing to be friendly. Then they'd think I was making trouble and might even stop me having taxis.

Everyone went off to work or school and Jack and I slept until about eleven o'clock. About midday, while I was fiddling around in the kitchen wondering what we could have to eat, there was a knock on the door. I picked up Jack to stop him getting into trouble, and went to answer it. Witch's Brew stood there with another woman – slim and smartly dressed, with short grey hair. The woman looked a bit taken-aback at the sight of Jack, then seemed to pull herself together.

Witch's Brew smiled at me chummily. 'This lady's looking for a man who fits the description of the man in your flat,' she said.

'I'm sorry to bother you,' the grey-haired woman said to me. 'I just really want to know if George Simpson lives here.'

I stared at her, recognising her voice from all the times she'd rung.

'Does he?' she asked again. 'You've just got to say yes or no.'

'Yes, he does,' Witch's Brew spoke up for me. 'Short bald man. That's your mum's new friend, isn't it?'

The woman tried to see past me. 'Is he in there now?'

I shook my head, not knowing whether to grass him up or not.

'He *does* live here, though? George Simpson?'

I nodded slightly.

The woman nodded. 'Ria saw him coming into these flats.'

Witch's Brew's eyes gleamed. 'I thought that was him. Neighbourhood Watch, see. You've got to keep an eye on your neighbours' comings and goings.'

'Are you George's wife?' I asked the woman.

'Yes, I am,' she said.

'And . . . you . . . want him back, do you?' I asked slowly.

'Certainly not!' she said, which took the wind out of my sails. 'Look, I don't want to involve you and your family, I just want a fair deal. I can't manage the mortgage on my own and George has taken the car and I'm finding it all very difficult.' She took a deep breath. 'I know where he works, of course, but I've got some official papers to serve on him and I need his home address.'

'39 Blenheim Court,' Witch's Brew said.

The woman nodded. 'Thanks. And you can tell your mother from me that this isn't the first time he's strayed.'

Witch's Brew stood by, hardly able to believe her luck, looking from me to the woman and back again.

'That's my lot with him, though. I've had enough now. You can also tell your mother that he's tight with money, has got a filthy temper and that she's welcome to him.'

'Right,' I said.

The woman turned and marched away and Witch's Brew winked at me. 'There!' she said. 'Well! All that glitters is not gold, eh? Tell your mum that.'

That afternoon, Jack was hot and bothered and very irritable, so I took him for a walk to buy the usual million and a half disposable nappies he used in a week – which took care of my allowance for the rest of the month. He seemed to be costing me more and more: his clothes were bigger now and so more expensive, he ate more food, wore larger nappies, needed all sorts of equipment. Luckily I'd had a cheque from my dad to pay for some of his winter clothes, otherwise it could all have got a bit hairy. Thinking about when he was older still worried me – what would I do when he wanted a bike and a computer and the right name trainers and all that stuff? With luck, though, I'd have a job by then. I'd have passed my A levels and be working somewhere nice, have good mates to go out with in the evenings and lots of money to spend on Jack and myself.

Mind you, where Jack was going to be while I was working and going out to these clubs I didn't know . . .

Soon, at least, we'd have more space, and that would be one problem solved. 'You're having your own room!' I said to Jack as I pushed him along. 'Jack's own room. Won't that be *lovely*!'

I pulled a funny face, trying to make him laugh, but Jack just looked up at me, bottom lip trembling. He wasn't himself; I could see that. Maybe he had a cold coming.

I turned my mind to other things. What was I going to say to George about his wife coming round? Should I say anything at all? If I didn't say anything, would he even find out she'd been? What about the messages she'd sent to Mum?

In the end, I decided not to say a word to either of them. I got the shopping and when I got back Ellie was in from school. I told *her* about George's wife of course, and she and I made a huge cauliflower cheese and giggled about what she'd said. When Mum and George came in from work we had the cauliflower with some fish fingers (George: 'I'm not used to these bits of meals. I'm used to meat and two veg.') and then they announced they had the keys to the new house and were going to have another look at it. Two days before, someone had put in an offer for our flat, so they were reasonably sure we *would* be moving.

'Oh, can Megan and I come?' Ellie asked straight away.

'We *are* going to be living there!' I said.

George shook his head impatiently. 'We can't all go. Five of us – it'd be like a bloody circus.' He looked at Jack, who had definitely started a cold now and was watery-eyed, with a runny nose. 'Can't you wipe that child's nose? He's putting me off my supper.'

'We can come and see the house, can't we, Mum?' I asked.

Mum looked at George. 'It would be all right, wouldn't it? The girls would love to see their rooms.'

He gave an exaggerated sigh. 'If you like. I suppose so.'

Quite excited, Ellie and I went to get ready. I changed Jack's nappy and wiped his face. He was all bunged up and his nose looked sore already; I hoped I wasn't going to have another bad night with him.

The house was empty. It was on the other side of town, about twenty years old, terraced, quite tall and on three floors. Downstairs there was a big kitchen and living room, you went up one set of stairs to two of the bedrooms and then up again for the other two. One of these rooms was tiny and had been done out by the previous owner as a study.

'George and I thought you and Jack could be up on this floor,' Mum said when we reached it, 'and our bedroom and Ellie's will be on the next floor down.'

'That way, with a bit of luck, we won't hear any noise from that child of yours,' George put in.

I fumed but kept quiet, not wanting to start a row what with it being our first time in the house.

The three of them went downstairs to look at their

own rooms and I stayed in the room which was going to be Jack's. There wasn't enough space for a wardrobe and it was painted a horrible dark green, *but it was his very own.*

'You in here. All on your own!' I said to him. 'I'm going to paint it buttercup yellow and you're going to have a proper bed and everything and you'll sleep all night.' I took him over to the window and looked down to the garden, which was long and narrow, with a tall fence right round and two trees in the centre of it. 'You can climb those trees,' I said. 'And you can have your duck down there with you to pull around, and ride one of those little bikes and play out there all the time.'

Jack rubbed his eyes and pushed his head into my neck, not interested. 'Just wait,' I said. 'You're going to love it.' I walked into what would be my room. My own room. By myself, that I wouldn't have to share with anyone. It was square and plain but it had a built-in wardrobe and enough space for a table. I could paint it what colours I liked and hang sari fabric at the window and it would be *brilliant.*

I could hear the others underneath, moving around, and then Ellie came running up the stairs, really excited. 'Won't it be fantastic!' she said. 'Have you seen the garden?' Before I replied she went on, 'George says you and I can share this shower up here and they can have the one on the middle floor all to themselves. Come down and see my room – I'm going to paint it green and silver and the ceiling is going to be purple.'

'Yuk,' I said.

'You won't be painting it those colours, young lady,' George said, appearing on the landing. 'I'm not having any house of mine rendered unsaleable.'

I looked at Ellie and rolled my eyes.

'And the ceilings will stay white, thank you very much.'

'Well,' Ellie faltered. 'I'm going to take the carpet up and have stripped pine floors – like they did on that homes programme.'

'That's what you think,' George said.

'Can't she do that?' we heard Mum ask.

'I don't want to be an old misery,' George said, as if he wasn't, 'but bare floorboards are blasted noisy. Get two people walking on them and it sounds like a herd of elephants.'

'Never mind,' I said in a low voice to Ellie. 'At least we can be away from them. We can get our own telly, stay in our rooms and let them get on with it.'

*

Jack was really grotty by the time we got home. I'd run out of clean tissues by then and his nose was running horribly, so that George shuddered as he held the car door open for us.

'Clean him up a bit, can't you?' he said, making a big thing about looking the other way.

'I will soon as we get in,' I said. 'Anyway, he can't help it.' Didn't your kids ever have colds? I wanted to ask.

When we went in there was a note on the mat from Mark. It said, *'What's wrong with your phone? Where are you all?'*

'Oooh!' Ellie wailed. 'We missed him.'

'He'll be back,' I said.

I went into the bathroom to run a bath, telling Mum I was going to bath Jack at the same time.

George, settling himself in front of the TV, said, 'Keep it to a few centimetres, will you? There's a water shortage.'

'What water shortage?' I said. 'I haven't seen anything in the papers.'

'Hot water costs money,' he said, 'and a bath takes a whole tank of hot water.'

I looked at Mum and raised my eyebrows. He was too much – and it was the second time that day he'd had a go at me about money. I'd phoned Claire earlier to give her our new number and tell her about the house and George had been standing by the phone tapping his fingers impatiently the whole time I was on. As it happened, I was glad to get off because all Claire had wanted to talk about was the holiday next April that three of them, Josie, Tina and her, were going on together, what a laugh they were going to have, what boys they were going to meet and how fantastic it was all going to be. I certainly hadn't wanted to hear *that*.

'At least Megan's bathing two for the price of one,' Mum said now.

George didn't answer. Mum went into the kitchen saying she was going to put the kettle on and I put Jack on the sitting-room floor with his duck.

Jack stopped grizzling for a moment and began to push the duck along, *quack-quack-quack*.

'D'you have to give him that duck?' George said. 'I can't hear myself think once that bloody thing starts.'

'It's only for a minute,' I said. 'It's just to keep him quiet while I get the bath ready.'

'And wipe his nose!'

'I just did.' I stared at George: it hadn't taken him

long to show what he was really like. It was no wonder that his wife had been glad to get rid of him, I thought, remembering that I'd never told him she'd been round. I went out of the room and started collecting stuff for our baths: towels and clean flannel, vest and sleeping suit for Jack, dressing gown for me, bubble bath and baby lotion for both of us. I turned off the bath water about an inch under my usual full-to-the-brim and went back into the sitting room to collect Jack. We'd both have a nice bath and play in the bubbles, and perhaps it would tire Jack out so that he would sleep soundly.

As I crossed the hall to get him, though, I heard him start screaming. I ran in – and Mum ran in from the kitchen, too – to see him lying on his back on the floor, yelling the place down.

'What happened?' I asked, snatching up Jack.

George shrugged. 'Nothing. He fell over, that's all. Lost his balance.'

I pressed Jack against me and rocked him.

'He's not hurt, is he,' George said. 'Only winded a bit.'

Jack screamed on while Mum examined his face. 'There are no cuts and bruises, Megan. He seems all right.'

I was too scared to look myself. 'Is he? Are you sure?'

'Not even a graze. You're all right, poppet, aren't you? Take him off, Megan. Give him his bath.'

I looked at George sitting there, one leg casually crossed over the other, reading the paper. His foot, balanced in the air, was just inches from where Jack had been sitting. It would only have taken him a moment to have kicked out and pushed Jack over. Maybe, if Jack had been grizzling continually, or making the duck quack too much . . . Maybe, if Jack had got on his nerves . . .

But maybe I was just being silly.

CHAPTER FOURTEEN

'That's fantastic!' Mark said. 'That's what you really need – some space and a room of your own.'

Mark and I were sitting on the sofa with Jack between us. Jack was 'reading' a board book, trying to find the duck he knew was on one of the pages. It was a week or so later – a Friday afternoon – and everything seemed to be going well with buying the new house.

'I bet Jack will sleep better on his own, too. Stands to reason – while you're all sleeping in the same room you must disturb each other.' Mark looked at me. 'What's this George like, then? I mean, not being funny but I can't imagine what sort of man your mum would go for.'

'I dunno,' I said, screwing up my face. 'I don't know what he's like really. He's one of those people you can't put your finger on.'

'An estate agent type, all mouth and trousers?' Mark asked.

I grinned. 'Yeah, a bit like that. Fine upstanding citizen sort of thing, always in a suit.'

'Good bloke? Funny?'

'Well, at first he was. Not funny, exactly, but jolly with us and talking about us being a proper family. Then as soon as he had his feet under the table he started changing, making comments about Jack being naughty and getting in digs about him never sleeping. And a couple of times he's really lost his temper.'

'With you?'

'With Jack.'

'*With Jack*?' Mark repeated, frowning.

'Ellie and I think he resents us. He'd rather have Mum all to himself.'

Mark shrugged. 'Par for the course, that is – but I don't like people who lose their tempers with babies. That's not good.'

I sighed. 'I know. I feel all mixed-up about it, really. I mean, things are much easier – shopping, for instance, and George can do stuff round the house, but I just don't like him. The thought of living with him in his own house! I mean, this place is Mum's and it's difficult, but the new place will be *his* and Mum's.'

'Hmm,' Mark said. 'You'll just have to take it

162

slowly, I guess. Living with someone for the first time is always difficult. So they say.'

'And he's got kids already. A boy and a girl. I've never heard that he's been to see them, though. I wonder how they feel about that.'

'Abandoned, I should think,' Mark said in a level voice. 'That's the word.' He went all quiet.

I gave him a push. 'It's not like *you*. You weren't abandoned.'

'Wasn't I?'

'Lorna didn't just go off and leave you without a thought. She spent ages worrying about what would be best for you, and crying about it and thinking about it.'

'Right,' he said.

I put my hand on his arm. 'Mark, honestly. She couldn't be more sorry. She feels terribly guilty about it. She told me she'd do anything to turn the clock back.' This drew no response so I added, 'She really, really loves you.'

'Yes, well . . . ' Mark said. He rested his chin on Jack's head.

'And she *did* do the best for you, didn't she? You had a good childhood and you get on great with your mum and dad, don't you?'

'That's not the point. Would you part with Jack? Ever?'

I shook my head. 'It was different in those days, though.'

'So you say.'

'She'd love to see more of you,' I persisted. 'Hasn't she asked you to go up there?'

He nodded.

'It would make her week . . . make her *century* if you did. I wish you would.'

'I'll see,' he said. He looked at his watch. 'I'd better go. I'm covering an author visit to the library this evening.'

'What have you got to do?'

He stood up. 'Well, it's not exactly hold the front page stuff – just take a photo of some famous old trout opening the new crime bookshelves.'

I stood up to go to the door with him. 'Ellie will kill me when she finds out she's missed you again.'

'Tell her I'll come over next week specially to see her. And I might see you one morning before that – OK?'

'OK.' I grinned. I'd told Mark about Mr Creep and he said he'd come along on one of our journeys, just to show him that I wasn't all alone in the world.

164

'How's the bloke who was chatting you up, by the way?'

'Jon?' I shook my head. 'Nothing to report. He was supposed to come and take me out but he didn't.'

Mark gave me a smacker of a kiss on the cheek. 'Never mind. Jack still loves you,' he said.

As I opened the front door, Ellie practically fell into our hall. It was only the fact that she was hanging on to Jamie which prevented her.

'Ah, now you can see Ellie *and* her boyfriend,' I said to Mark, grinning.

'He's not a boyfriend!' Ellie said. She dropped her arms from around Jamie's neck. 'I didn't know you were here,' she said, flustered.

'See, you'd have seen Mark if you'd come straight home from school like a good girl,' I said, 'with no snogging on the way,' I added in an undertone.

'Shut up!' she hissed at me.

'So this is your not-boyfriend, is it?' Mark said. 'And there's me thinking you were saving yourself for me.'

Jamie disappeared with a 'See you,' and Ellie never even glanced after him. 'Oh, don't go. Stay and talk to me,' she said to Mark. 'I'll play you my new CD.'

'Can't do it, love,' he said. 'I've got an important

press call.' He winked at me. 'I'll see you both next week. Right?'

He went off and Ellie gazed down the corridor after him. 'Gorgeous or what,' she breathed.

That evening, after Jack had gone to bed, Mum got out some paint charts and George said we could choose what colours we wanted for our rooms, because apparently the firm of decorators that the estate agents used were going to paint them before we moved in. Ellie and I looked at each other, pleased. Maybe he'd relented and we could have buttercup yellow and green and silver after all.

And then we looked at the paint charts. 'Out of *these*?' I said, looking at the colours on the card. 'They're white, white and off-white. I can hardly see any difference between them.'

'They're all neutrals,' George said. 'Pale, restful colours.'

Ellie nudged me to say something.

'Why can't we have our rooms proper colours? Bright colours?' I asked.

George shook his head. 'Because, with your neutrals, it's easier if you want to change your décor and the colour of your duvet and so on. Also it's better when it comes to selling again.'

'But I wanted a nice bright yellow for Jack's room,' I said.

'This one here's called daffodil white,' Mum said. 'It's *quite* yellow.'

'Hardly,' I said witheringly. I was tired and fed up and now I couldn't even have Jack's bedroom the colour I wanted it. 'I'm not asking for it to be bright red or anything – just yellow! That's not exactly out-landish, is it?'

Mum shot a look at George. It was funny, I'd always thought of her as a bold, outspoken sort of woman, but since George had come on the scene she'd gone a bit fluffy. She didn't seem to have opin-ions of her own any more.

'We'll see later, perhaps – after we've moved in,' she said to me.

'No, we won't!' George said. 'I don't want either of the girls decorating their own rooms and making a mess of them. We're moving to a nice house in a nice area and I want to make sure it stays that way.'

Mum looked at Ellie and me and said, kind-of like an apology, 'George and I are sinking all our money into this house.'

'So?'

'It's not fair!' Ellie said. 'We ought to be allowed to have what colours we want for our own bedrooms!'

'Well, you're not,' George said. 'And just count yourself lucky you're coming to this house at all.'

Ellie gave a little gasp at this and I bit my lip and looked over to Mum, wanting her to say something. She didn't though, so I just gave George a hate-filled glare and got up and went into the bedroom, creeping in quietly so as not to wake Jack.

'Pig!' I muttered to myself. 'Fat pig.'

I laid down on my bed. I hated him – but what did that matter? Mum liked him, Mum wanted him and in time, I expected that Mum would marry him. And if I fell out with him I would find myself living in a horrible B and B somewhere.

I hadn't said anything to anyone about Jack falling over the other evening. I just wasn't sure enough. Jack might have been on the floor by accident: he *did* fall and roll over a lot, and somehow it was easier to think that this was what had happened. If I started to question this, came to believe George *had* kicked him, then I'd have to do something about it.

What, I didn't know. Mum more than likely wouldn't believe me, would think I was only saying it because I didn't get on with George. If I told someone else – who? Vicky? – she might get the Social Services down to ask me a whole lot of questions, and they might say that Jack and I had to be separated from George, and put me somewhere grotty. Worse – *horrendous* – they might think that Jack wasn't safe and take him away from me.

Ellie crept into the bedroom. 'They're having a row!' she whispered.

'What about?'

'Something about a holiday next year. They're going and we're not.'

'Oh, thanks a bundle, George,' I muttered.

'Not that we want to go anyway. Not with him,' Ellie said.

'What did Mum say?'

'Something about it would be lovely for Jack at the seaside, and then *he* said he wasn't providing holidays for all and sundry, that they needed some time on their own, without kids. Then he said that he wasn't going to pay for us, and that if she felt Jack ought to go to the seaside then his father or grandfather could take him and pay for him, because he certainly wasn't going to.'

'Pig!' I muttered under my breath. I wanted to rush in there and say it but I didn't dare. I sat up, rocking backwards and forwards on the bed. I felt frustrated and full of fury. I had no money, no power, no voice that anyone would listen to. 'Life stinks!' I said to Ellie.

'You bet it does,' she said.

CHAPTER FIFTEEN

'It was the bloody solicitors at the door!' George said, marching into the kitchen and flinging a long brown envelope on to the breakfast table. 'Served the papers on me personally, they did. Took me unawares.'

We'd all been dashing about having our bits of breakfast when the front-door bell had gone, long and loud. I'd been settling Jack into his high chair and Mum had been doing something with Ellie, so George had gone to answer it.

'Bloody solicitors. Parasites,' he spat out.

'Is it the divorce papers?' Mum asked.

George swore loudly by way of reply and sat down again, throwing the envelope on to the table and knocking over a jug of milk. Jack, startled by the sudden crash and confusion, started to cry.

'Oh, that's all we need,' George said, '*him* starting. As if crying all night isn't enough.'

'Sssh. Never mind,' Mum said, beginning to clear up the mess.

'You frightened him – that's why he started crying,' I said.

George shot him a look which said, *I'll give him something to be frightened about.*

'And don't look at him like that!' I said immediately. 'It's all right,' I said to Jack. I smoothed his hair out of his face. It was getting long; he was going to need a haircut soon. 'It's all right, darling.'

'Look, calm down, everyone,' Mum said. She put her hand on George's shoulder. 'What do you have to do about those papers?'

'I don't know,' George said irritably. 'I don't even know what they are. I'm not going to open them.'

'You'll have to!' Mum said.

'Yes, all right, I'll have to *some* time,' he said. 'I'm just not going to do it now.'

Jack stopped crying and I spooned more cereal into his mouth. He could feed himself now, after a fashion, but I liked to do it if it was anything messy or we were just about to go out. All the time he was chomping he kept a wary eye on George.

Ellie went off to school and then just as George and Mum were about to leave for work, the front-door bell went again.

'You can go,' George said to me. 'And if it's anyone official, I'm not here.'

It was Mark. I brought him in, and Jack beamed at him. 'Up!' he said, holding up his arms to be lifted.

'Another word!' Mum and I said together. Mum gave Mark a kiss and introduced him to George, who barely gave him the time of day.

I wiped around Jack's mouth, got him out of his chair and handed him to Mark. 'You've missed Ellie,' I said, 'so can you amuse him for five minutes instead?'

I dashed round collecting things and a couple of minutes later Mum and George went off to work. Mark came to find me.

'I see what you mean about George,' he said. 'Not exactly oozing charm, is he?'

'He's in a really bad mood,' I said. 'Some papers arrived from a solicitor. Something about his divorce.'

We went into the kitchen and Mark looked hopefully at the teapot. 'Have I got time for a cuppa?'

'Only just.' I passed him a clean mug. 'Have you come here to go for a ride in the taxi with me?'

He nodded, grinning.

'You won't say anything about . . . you know, what he said, will you?' I asked anxiously. 'Only I've got to

173

go in that cab with him for the rest of the term.'

Mark poured himself a mug of lukewarm, stewed tea with one hand and balanced Jack on his knee with the other. 'I've got it all planned,' he said. 'Leave it to me.' He took a swig of tea, pulled a face, and then asked casually, 'By the way, have you got a coach timetable?'

'Where for? Where're you going?'

'Chester,' he said, all deadpan.

I stopped what I was doing, amazed. '*Really*? You're going to see Lorna?'

'Might,' he said.

'Brilliant!' I felt a big lump come in my throat. 'Oh, Mark, that's fantastic . . . '

'I just said I might,' he said. 'Don't get all excited.'

'You *will*, though, won't you?'

He shrugged. 'I suppose so. I've been thinking about what you said. I reckon I really ought to give her a chance to explain, give her side of the story sort of thing. Maybe when I can understand the circumstances . . . '

I took a deep breath. '*Fantastic*,' I said again. I didn't want to get all bunged up with crying – not with ordeal by taxi driver coming up – so I tried to compose myself. 'Just for that,' I said, 'I'm going to make you a fresh cup of tea.'

*

174

Mr Creep arrived as usual, pulling into the layby where Jack, Mark and I were waiting.

'I've got an extra passenger, if that's all right,' I said to him. 'This man's a reporter from the local newspaper.'

He looked startled. 'Oh. What's he in aid of then?'

I smiled sweetly. 'I'll let him tell you that.'

Mark had Jack on one arm and was carrying his changing bag in the other, together with his own camera and gadget bag. I had my usual bundles and bags and stuff.

'Could you give us a hand, old chap?' Mark asked pleasantly.

The driver hesitated.

'It's a bit difficult with the baby and all,' Mark added. 'That'd be great if you could.'

Mr Creep was spurred into action. 'Certainly,' he said.

'I expect you're wondering what I'm here for,' Mark began when we were all settled in and he was about to move off.

The driver's eyes looked shiftily at me and I could see he was wondering what was coming next.

'What it is – I'm hoping to do a regular piece for the local paper. It's going to be called *Familiar Faces*.'

'Oh yes?'

'It'll feature local people who are working in the community: nurses, milkmen, postmen, taxi drivers . . . people who make a difference to our everyday lives. People who do a service or who help others in some way.'

The driver nodded warily.

'I want to make you a bit of a star!' Mark went on. 'I'll take down some details and write a little piece on you. Perhaps you can give me some stories about the sort of people you help in your day-to-day life.' He smiled pleasantly. 'Because I'm sure you do help people who perhaps don't have the advantages that you have. And then I'll take a few photographs of you in your cab – and perhaps one of you helping this young lady with her stuff at the other end. Just to give readers the flavour of the job.'

'Oh. Right,' Mr Creep said, settling back in his seat. He smiled rather smugly. 'I'm going to be a star, am I?'

'It might not appear in the paper for a month or so, of course – not until I've got half a dozen other interviews under my belt. And during that time I'll be in touch with this young lady . . . ' He turned to me. 'Sorry, what did you say your first name was again?'

'Megan,' I said, deadpan.

'I'll be in touch with Megan to find out if there have been any changes in circumstances,' Mark said. He paused. 'If you see what I mean.'

'Right,' the driver said. 'Okey doke.'

Mark nudged me and I nudged him back, and then we both stared out of our respective windows or made polite conversation as if we'd never met before in our lives.

I left them outside Poppies. Mark was setting things up to shoot some pictures and the driver was posing in his cab, smiling fatly and falsely. I grinned to myself: Mark was *brilliant*!

About noon, when some of us were in the nursery giving our babies their lunch, I had another visitor.

'Guess who?' someone said, putting their hand on my shoulder, and I turned and Kirsty was standing there smiling at me. She looked much better, her hair clean and shiny and her face smiley instead of strained. She had Stella with her in a little straw carrycot.

'You've come back!' I gave her a hug and I looked at Stella. 'And Stella's back as well. How are you getting on?'

'All right,' Kirsty said. 'Fine!' She sat down,

breathing happiness. 'I got her back two days ago. They've done all the tests and there's nothing wrong with her – they've just changed her milk formula.' She moved the plaid blanket in the cot so that I could see Stella better. 'Look! Isn't she beautiful?'

I nodded. 'Lovely!' She did look lovely: her eyes were shiny bright, her cheeks pink and her hair brushed and fluffy.

Kirsty heaved a blissful sigh, gazing down at her. 'I've got her back! I was really worried they wouldn't let me have her.'

'It's brilliant,' I said. I looked to see if she had her books with her. 'Have you come back here for a class?'

She shook her head. 'Only to see you and the girls. Vicki hasn't been able to arrange a taxi run yet because I'm out of the area. It took me three buses! I couldn't come every day.'

'Are you still at the foster mother's place? How is it?'

'It's OK now. She's not a bad old stick.' Kirsty smiled. 'I get on better with her than I did with my own mum, actually.'

'And are you allowed to stay there with her?'

She nodded. 'Until I'm eighteen. Then I'll get a

flat.' She pointed at Jack – while I was talking to Kirsty he'd taken the opportunity to creep up on little Lloyd and pinch a crisp. 'Isn't he walking well! What's been happening to you, then?'

'Oh, you know,' I said. 'Celeb parties, clubs, a Barbados beach holiday – the usual things. But we're going to move soon. That's quite exciting.'

'You and Jack?' she asked, surprised.

'I wish. Me and my mum and sister – and my mum's bloke. We're moving from our flat to a house nearby. Jack's going to have his own bedroom and so am I.'

'Brilliant!' Kirsty said. 'Perhaps I can come over and see you.'

''Course you can,' I said, squashing the thought of what George would say about *two* babies in the house. 'Come any time you like.'

Later that afternoon, as I went along the corridor to the flat, the phone was ringing. It stopped just as I put my key in the lock.

'Missed it! See you tomorrow?' said Mr Creep – who had actually come with me, *up to the door* – carrying Jack's little chair and some large, messy red and blue 'paintings' that he'd done that day.

'Yes, thanks,' I said, hiding a grin. 'Thank you for your help.'

'Not at all,' he said, trying to outdo me in politeness.

By the time I was indoors with all my stuff the phone was ringing again. I put Jack on the floor and picked it up.

'Told you I'd ring,' a voice said. It was Jon.

'I can't really talk now,' I said, and was pleased with myself. I could be cool because I'd given up hope of him ever ringing; had trained myself not to think about him. 'I've only just come through the door and I've got a million things to do.'

'Aaah, that's a shame, because I was going to chat you up,' Jon said.

I heard a crash as Jack reached the kitchen cupboard and pulled out the saucepans. 'Well, you can if you're quick about it,' I said.

'So what's the hurry?'

'If you must know – we've got the people coming round who're buying this flat,' I said. 'And I promised my mum I'd make the beds.'

'Where are you moving to, then?'

I told him and he said it was much nearer to where he lived. 'So I'll be able to see you properly.'

'Maybe,' I said, thinking that I wasn't going to get too excited.

'What I was thinking about was us going out on a Saturday during the day. We could go into town, take a walk, have a bite to eat.'

'When?' I asked guardedly.

'Next Saturday? I could meet you in town. By the station, say.'

'Can I bring Jack?' I asked. 'He likes going for walks.' I didn't *have* to bring Jack, I might have been able to leave him with Ellie, but it was a test.

'Mmm,' Jon said.

'What's that mean?'

'It means I'm thinking about it. It wasn't what I had in mind, quite honestly.'

'What did you have in mind, then?' From the kitchen I heard a rhythmic *bang-bang-bang* as Jack crashed two lids together.

'Well, I was thinking of walking you back to my place. I've got the house to myself for the weekend.'

'Aaah,' I said, and red *DANGER* flags started flapping in my head. 'That's not a walk and a bite to eat, is it? I don't think so.'

'Why not?'

'I hardly know you.'

'So? I'm not suggesting anything. Just an afternoon to ourselves and a chat, that's all.'

'Sorry,' I said. 'I haven't got anyone to look after Jack, and a jolly day out with a baby obviously isn't what you had in mind.'

There was a silence – apart from all the noise from Jack – and then Jon said, 'Well, if you change your mind.'

'Sure,' I said. 'Otherwise – see you.'

'See you,' he echoed.

But it was obvious that I wouldn't.

CHAPTER SIXTEEN

When George came in, he was still in a bad mood. I didn't care, though, because I was in a bad mood, too. Mostly this was because what Mark and Michelle had both warned me of had turned out to be right. Jon, spelled J-O-N, was only after one thing. Was everyone, I wondered? Was I ever going to meet someone who wasn't? Why didn't someone love me obsessively and blindly and passionately, like Heathcliff had loved Cathy? Or didn't people love other people like that any more?

'That child's table manners are appalling,' George said when we were in the kitchen having tea.

'Give him a chance,' I said. 'He's only just started to feed himself.'

As Jack gnawed on a piece of half-chewed rusk, dribble all down his face, George looked away in disgust. 'Perhaps in the new house, children's mealtimes could be at a different time from those of adults.'

'When you first came you wanted us all to eat

together,' I pointed out. 'And anyway, Jack's had his tea. I'm just keeping him quiet with that rusk.'

Mum said, 'Oh come on, George – Jack's not that bad. And children grow up so quickly.'

'One of *yours* has had a child of her own before she's grown up!' George retorted. 'It means we – you and I – have got to raise two generations.'

'No, you haven't,' I said, 'I'll be getting my own place as soon as I possibly can.'

'That's enough!' Mum said. 'Now, I've bought an apple crumble. Custard or ice cream with it?'

After we'd eaten Ellie went off to her friend's house to watch a video and I decided to write to Luke – Jack's daddy – and send him some of the latest photos of his son. Luke might not be earning any money now but when he'd finished at uni he would, and I wanted to make sure Jack was in with a chance when it came to getting some.

I went to rummage around in my bedroom for some decent writing paper, leaving Mum and George in the kitchen discussing what to say about moving dates to the people who were buying the flat. Jack was in the sitting room with some of his toys and I was going to try to keep him awake until the buyers had been.

Finding a writing pad took longer than I thought, so I was away from him for five or six minutes. Witch's Brew called, wanting to talk to Mum about when we were moving, and Mum was still at the door chatting to her when I heard a noise like a slap – well, it *was* a slap – and George saying, 'Get off, you bloody kid!'

I ran into the sitting-room. George was standing by the window and Jack was on the floor with some screwed up paper beside him. Jack look startled, pale and shocked.

'What have you done?' I shouted at George, and I snatched up Jack. Lifting him suddenly made him take in a great gasp of air so that he began screaming.

'What have you done?' I shouted again at George. I looked carefully along Jack's arms, face and legs and then I saw it: on his bare leg was a red weal, a raised handprint. 'You beast! You've really hurt him!' I said, and began crying myself.

'He deserved it. Look what he's done!' George said, his voice shaking with rage. 'He – that blasted child – got into my briefcase. He's destroyed some important legal documents that arrived this morning.'

'So?'

'So he's got to be taught. Got to understand the meaning of the word "no".'

'He's just a baby! How . . . how dare you smack him! He's *my* baby. He's nothing to do with you!'

'Is that right? Nothing to do with me? How come I'm paying for his food and clothing and the roof over his head, then?'

There was no answer to this and I just stood there, Jack sobbing on my shoulder, frightened and hurt. Mum came in from the hall. 'What on earth's going on? Why are you two rowing again?'

'He hit Jack!' I said.

'It was just a smack,' George said. 'The child got into my briefcase – destroyed some important papers. It was an instinctive reaction.'

'You smacked him?' Mum asked.

'I gave him a bit of a fright, that's all,' George said. 'It was nothing. He was crying before he was hurt.'

I hugged Jack to me, tears running down my cheeks. My mind was going full-pelt but I was aware that there was a whole lot at stake here. If I spoke now, said what I ought to, everything could change. I stood to lose my precious new room, and Jack's room, too. The space, privacy and new life I'd been so looking forward to might never happen.

I brushed away the tears. 'Oh, he hit him all right,'

I said to Mum, and I carried Jack over to her to show her the red weal.

Mum gasped. 'You did this?' she asked George.

'I told you – the kid's got to learn.'

'And that's not all,' I said. 'You kicked him the other day, didn't you? I wasn't sure at first, but I am now.'

'What rubbish,' George blustered.

'You did. And he's terrified of you. That's why he always plays up when you're around.'

Jack took in a great shuddering breath, resting his head on my shoulder. I felt my anger rise again. 'If you ever . . . ever . . . touch him again I'll kill you!' I said.

There was a long silence and then Mum said, rather shakily, 'I don't believe it.'

My heart sank. I felt sick. 'You don't believe it! How can you say that?' I cried. 'Who d'you think made that big mark on his leg, then?'

'Oh, I believe George did it,' Mum said quietly. 'I just can't believe it of *him*. For a man to hit a *baby* . . . '

George looked shifty. 'OK, I maybe tapped him a bit hard,' he said. 'What's all the fuss about?'

'Mum . . . ' I pleaded. Don't let me down, Mum, I said silently.

'It won't happen again,' George said.

'No, it won't.' Mum held out her arms for Jack and

187

I let her take him and cuddle him. After a moment she said, 'I'm sorry, George,' in a very calm and reasonable voice.

'What d'you mean – you're sorry? What's that supposed to mean?'

'I'm sorry but I won't be moving into that house with you after all.'

My eyes filled with fresh tears. *Oh, cheers, Mum . . .*

'But . . . but we're buying it together,' George said. 'We're engaged.'

'No, we're not,' Mum said, twisting off the ring and pushing it towards him. 'I'm sorry but I couldn't live with you. You're not the man I thought you were. My first duty is to my children, and if I can't trust you with them, then that's the end of it.'

'I don't believe I'm hearing this!' George shouted. 'I've left my wife for you! I'm buying a house with you – helping you out of this pigsty!'

Mum smiled a little. 'We've been living in this pigsty quite happily up to now, and we can go on living in it.'

'You're doing a stupid thing, Christine,' George said warningly. 'We've got a good life ahead of us – don't let this little thing spoil it.'

'This isn't a little thing,' Mum said. 'Anyone who

comes into my life must love my children – and Jack – as much as I do. If they don't then it's no good. No good at all.'

George got up and started swearing and pacing about angrily.

'Perhaps you'd better go and pack now,' Mum said after a moment. 'Go back to your wife if she'll have you.' He went to say something and she turned away from him and said, cold and distant, 'I've made up my mind, George. Don't bother to try and say another word.'

She didn't say anything after that, but she and I sat down on the sofa together, with Jack hugged between us, while George raved, swore a bit, then had another go at Mum. Eventually he went into the bedroom and must have started packing.

I think he got as far as putting one suitcase outside the door ready to take and then the new people turned up to see the flat again. I don't know what he said to them because I could only hear the murmur of voices, but after a while they went away.

And then he went away as well and Mum and I just sat there for ages. In the end Jack went to sleep on my lap and Mum gave a couple of nervous coughs and said, 'I'm sorry, Megan.'

'What for?'

'Sorry about George and everything. I thought it would be OK. I really thought we might be able to make a go of it but I . . . ' She shook her head and sighed. 'I put Jack in jeopardy and could have ruined all our lives.'

I put my cheek on Jack's downy head and she went on. 'This might sound odd and you may not be able to understand it at your age, but I thought George was my last hope. I'd more or less given up on having a proper relationship with anyone ever again. George – well, thinking about it now, I probably rather grabbed at him without working things through. All I could see was a husband, car and decent income – *and* a proper house – somewhere we could bring up Jack together.'

I nodded slowly.

'Then as soon as he moved in – and believe me, that situation was forced on me much sooner than I would have chosen – I began to see the drawbacks. But I told myself that once we were in the new house with all the space and everything, it would be all right.' She shook her head. 'It wouldn't have been, of course.'

I didn't say anything – I didn't know what to say – but I patted her hand. I mean, we aren't a very touchy-feely family, but right then I felt pretty close to her. I knew that she'd chosen us over him, and was grateful. I knew, too, the answer to that constant question about who I was. Before anything else, first and foremost, I was a mum. And if the time ever came when I had to decide between Jack and someone else, then it would always be Jack.